Also by Naomi A. Hintze

YOU'LL LIKE MY MOTHER
THE STONE CARNATION

ALOHA MEANS GOODBYE

Random House New York

ALOHA
MEANS
GOODBYE

by Naomi A. Hintze

Library of Congress Cataloging in Publication Data
Hintze, Naomi A.
Aloha means goodbye.
I. Title.
PZ4.H665Al   [PS3558.I55]   813'.5'4   72–37049
ISBN 0–394–48028–7

Manufactured in the United States of America
by The Book Press, Brattleboro, Vt.
98765432

For Laea and Kwan Yan Au

ALOHA MEANS GOODBYE

CHAPTER ONE

It had been a very long night. Sara Moore on her high, narrow bed was relieved to see that morning light was turning the windows gray, restoring a tint of yellow to the walls. Down the hall, off and on all night, a woman had screamed. Now there was no screaming. Perhaps the woman was in less pain, or she was sedated, or she had died. No use asking. The nurses never would tell you anything. They must take courses in Bright Smiling and Noncommittal Answers.

Sara closed her eyes, although she knew there was no point in trying to sleep now. This day would begin earlier than usual, for she was scheduled to have the last of her tests, a heart catheterization. There was nothing alarming about it, Dr. Durham had assured her. He would come by this morning to explain the procedure.

She adored Dr. Durham. Since he was a widower, sometimes

the nurses liked to pretend they thought she had a romantic interest in him. He was as old as her father, though he looked much older with his thinning gray crew cut and a slight paunch. Chief of Hematology, he had taken a special interest in her ominous array of symptoms since she had first come to the hospital in early April. He told her the truth even at the beginning when it had seemed the diagnosis might be a bad one. He always answered every question in as much detail as she desired.

When Sara had been scheduled for a sternal puncture he had agreed calmly enough that the idea of boring into her breastbone for samples of marrow sounded grisly. "But a look at your bone cells is essential if we are to rule out certain possibilities. You may have a twinge when the marrow is aspirated—I promise it won't bother you much. I think I can also promise you that an evaluation of those cells won't reveal any abnormalities."

Her illness had begun with a bad sore throat and high fever in early spring. Her joints were sore and her glands swollen. A baffled family physician had sent her down here to Brill Hospital in St. Louis, and for five weeks the consultations and testings had gone on. By now the file of Miss Sara Moore, age twenty-five, was crammed with charts and case history, including childhood diseases, family allergies, details of her mother's single pregnancy, and what all four grandparents had died of. Her blood—B-negative, rare—had been spun in a centrifuge, smeared on slides, peered at through microscopes, with cells and platelets counted. Every inmost organ had been probed, X-rayed; glands had been biopsied and soon they would be able to look at all the hieroglyphics and percentages and say, This is Sara Moore.

Important details necessary to the understanding of Sara Moore, though properly omitted from medical records, would have included the information that she had mouse-blond hair, a few freckles, and sky-blue eyes. Her face with its delicate prettiness had a still look much of the time that imitated serenity and denied fantasies and hopes. She was five feet four inches, with a figure that was, in spite of its economical dimensions, noticeably better than average.

She had parents who loved her and whom she loved, a pleasant home in a pleasant if dying Illinois town. With only two years of college, she was unable to get a real teaching job, but she enjoyed well enough what she did at Miss Janey's nursery school. She thumped the piano, ran in the play yard, zipped and unzipped, wiped tears, noses and bottoms, and loved in varying degrees every child who came under her care. One afternoon a week she worked as a volunteer at the County Home for the Aged. Sara Moore, anybody would have told you, was the nicest girl in town.

The top of the hospital bureau was reduced now to a few potted plants and some Peace roses Dr. Durham had brought in yesterday, but during her first few weeks it had been crowded with flowers. The nurses marveled as they bore the overflow to other rooms, but when they came to know her they understood. Sara was sweet, always cheerful and undemanding; she never pushed her call button.

Deep inside her, unsuspected by anyone who knew her, invisible to X-ray and perhaps eventually to be silenced like that woman down the hall, was a girl who screamed. A rude girl, careless of the feelings of others, not wanting to be loved by everybody. A girl who said, Who the hell wants to be the nicest girl in town?

Sara turned on the narrow bed, trying to warm feet that had been cold for five weeks. In her dreams she slept warmly on a king-sized bed, held close by a shaggy-haired young man whom she had never seen in waking life.

Tears surprised her. She never cried.

CHAPTER TWO

The door opened and a nurse marched in. It was Mrs. Harr, of the old yellowed hair and aggressive teeth. "Good morning, good morning, good morning!" determined that it should be so. Mrs. Harr must have received, years ago, an A-plus in Bright Smiling. Her every movement suggested that mere years would never dim her exuberance.

Sara gave a furtive swipe to her eyes, knowing that her tears would go on her daily chart.

"Oh, I do feel so *good* when I come on duty every morning. Especially when it's a lovely morning like this morning. I am just *crazy* about these first warm days, aren't you?"

"Yes," said Sara.

"I love to get up early and attack the day." She laughed loudly, her teeth looking as if they might be about to take a large, cheerful bite of it. She seized the thermometer with an excess of energy that could have lifted an iron bar, and held it toward Sara.

Sara opened her mouth, closed it on the slim tube's alcohol taste.

"Look at those roses over there. My, my, I bet I know who brought you those. And guess what *I* brought you—" The fingers of one hand were on Sara's wrist, and her other hand went into her pocket. "Another contest entry blank. It's got your lucky number right on it and you don't have to buy a thing."

Around the thermometer Sara said, "What do I not win this time?"

Mrs. Harr finished counting Sara's pulse and wrote it down. "What an attitude! Now, Sara, every time you enter a contest you must say to yourself, This time I'm going to win. *This* time it's a boat you're going to win."

"Good. Swell. Thank you. Put it over there on that stack with the rest of them."

"Everybody in the hospital has been bringing these to you, I know. You just fill them all out, and this summer when you're all well you can sail in your boat, wearing that mink jacket you filled out a blank for when you first came in, flashing your diamond ring, and playing your tape machine with—what was it? —a year's supply of free tapes?" She threw back her head with a wide laugh.

Mrs. Harr always gave Sara a small relapse. She smiled dutifully.

Still laughing at her witticism, Mrs. Harr took out the thermometer, peered at it, and wrote down the temperature. "Now, then, I want you to take off your nightgown and put on this snappy little number for me. No breakfast for you this morning, I guess you know that. Just some more of that lovely stuff they gave you when you had your sternal puncture. There, now, let me help you tie these tapes. Say, how come a nice girl like you"— Sara braced herself—"isn't married?"

If there was an answer to that Sara hadn't found it.

Mrs. Harr eyed her as she picked up the hypodermic syringe that lay ready with its swab of cotton. "Bet you're Daddy's girl. I could tell that when your parents were here the other day. They're both lovely, but that father of yours looks like a big, gangling high school boy."

"He's a high school principal. It kills my mother that he looks so young, but she's fighting it with all she's got—exercises, diets—" She held up the sleeve of her coarse white gown, felt the coolness of the alcohol, the thrust of the needle. Mrs. Harr gave shots with such a joyous stab that they could scarcely be felt. "Hold it right there!" she shouted, and was off in search of her next victim.

Sara was still holding the cotton swab on her arm when Dr. Durham walked in. His relaxed manner was a relief. He looked at her chart that hung on the end of her bed and then came to smile down at her, his eyes a benevolent brown. "How's our girl this morning? Slept well, I hope? No qualms?"

"No qualms"—it was easy to smile at him—"now that you're here to tell me what they're going to do."

"Well, you've had your Demerol and scopolamine." He drew a chair up to her bed. "Your mouth will be a little dry, but it's a great combination. Has an amnesic effect, makes the whole thing dreamlike. You will be conscious, but you won't remember much, won't worry. Within the hour they'll come and take you down to what we call the Cath Lab—it's like an operating room."

"Will you be there?"

"You bet. Somebody else will be doing the job, but I'll be standing by."

"Good. I'll feel better if you're there. Then what?"

"First they will inject a little procaine in the groin area so you won't feel anything. Then they will make a tiny nick to the femoral vein so the catheter can be inserted. It's very pliable, like a piece of the thinnest cooked spaghetti, and it will be pushed up very gently to enter your heart. Dye will be injected and X-rays will be made, dozens of them. You'll hear a *boom, boom, boom* sound as the film cassettes change for rapid sequence. I'll be watching the screen."

"Will you be able to tell then if anything is wrong?"

"Yes. We'll do a thorough study later, but I expect to be able to see right away that your heart is okay. This is just one last test, Sara, that I feel should be made. You came in here with a scary bunch of symptoms, little girl. We had a choice of some pretty frightening diseases—Hodgkins, leukemia, aplastic anemia, lymphosarcoma, multiple myeloma—and one by one we've ruled them all out. I've seen your cells and they're beautiful. I think after this test we're going to be able to send you home with a clean bill of health."

"I am beginning to feel floaty."

"Good. You just float on down to the Cath Lab." He patted her hand and got up. "See you there."

He was a darling guy, paunch and all.

It could have been only minutes later or it could have been an hour when she was moved to a stretcher, strapped down and whirled on rubber tires along halls, down on an elevator, and brought to rest in another hall. She closed her eyes, pleasantly groggy, very peaceful. The orderly said something about parking her there for a minute while he went into the lab to see if they were ready for her.

Sara meant to say, Take your time, but she couldn't quite get out the words with her dry lips. Odd that her mouth should be so dry when she wasn't thirsty.

It sounded as if two men whispered over her head. "Is this the girl?"

"Yes, this is the girl."

"Is she—?"

Is she—what? Dead? In a minute she would manage to look up and startle them.

"She seems so young. Is she . . . you're sure?"

"Oh, yes. I've seen all the records. She hasn't a chance."

Sara forced her eyes open. She looked up and saw only the blur of retreating shapes. With an effort, strapped down as she was, she twisted around as best she could. Several people walked along the hall, some of them doctors and nurses. An orderly pushed racks of rattling bottles.

Me? Not a chance?

How very curious. She would have to think about this when her brain was a little clearer. She supposed that she would care a little.

Her orderly was back and the stretcher was floating again. Just a little way this time around a lovely, whirly corner and into a room that was like an operating room and which was, she supposed, what Dr. Durham had called the Cath Lab.

She saw what looked like several plain, ordinary television sets. As she was moved from the stretcher to the operating table she noticed a large screen behind her, over her head.

Figures in green. Half a dozen of them. Some of them had on bulky aprons and huge black gloves. The black gloves caused a song to play itself in her head: "Mickey Mouse . . . Mickey Mouse . . ." It was the tune from the TV show she used to watch when she was a little girl. She felt as carefree now as she had then.

One of the figures, brown-eyed, pulled his mask down and Dr. Durham smiled at her. "Feeling good?"

She tried to wet her lips to say she felt great, but there was no saliva. She smiled and nodded.

Suspended over her was a huge piece of X-ray equipment that looked as if it weighed a ton. She saw something round with a reflecting surface like a mirror.

Another doctor leaned, his eyes crinkling. "Hi. I'm Dr. Levinson. I'll be in charge, so blame me if anything tickles. This really is a very candid camera, so remember to smile."

She had the feeling he had said those words to hundreds of patients. She knew she was expected to smile at his joke, so she smiled.

"You shouldn't have very much discomfort. We're going to inject the procaine now—you'll feel the prick of the needle."

They avoided the word "pain." They didn't trust you with it. They preferred "twinge," "prick," "tickle." Nobody ever said, This will hurt like hell. Her mind spun off for a bit.

Some swabbing had been going on in the groin area. A barely perceptible sting or two then, seeming scarcely to do with her flesh at all. An exchange of instruments. Words murmured behind the masks. Intent sets of eyes peering down.

"This looks like the vein—yes. There, we've got the catheter in now. Inject. Start the pictures." Eyes were lifted to look into a round, reflecting surface.

A loud and rapid *boom, boom* at her head startled her until she remembered it had something to do with the changing of the film cassettes.

"Beautiful . . . So far the right side looks fine . No septal defects . . . Vessels to lungs look normal. Turn her now just a little."

Something hurt. Sara frowned and the brown eyes leaned. "Got to take a look at the left side too, Sara. That little poke is all you're going to feel. Okay now? Everything is looking fine."

But those men said I hadn't a chance. Were they doctors?

Nobody answered or seemed to hear. She wasn't sure whether she had said the words out loud.

Their words were overlapping: *Lucky girl. Everything's perfect. No problems.*

So the whispering voices had been wrong.

The booming had stopped. The tubing was being withdrawn. Stitches now, she supposed. Painless with the procaine still doing its job.

Back in her room again, Sara lay flat with a sandbag on the area of the small incision. She was thirsty now, but had been given only ice to suck since water might cause nausea. She had the feeling that she had been through a dream, interesting, not unpleasant.

Dr. Durham came in beaming.

Sara held up her hand, ready with her question. "One minute before you say anything. I heard somebody down there say I hadn't a chance."

The smile faded. "What are you talking about? Who said that?"

"I don't know. It sounded like two men were whispering over my head as I lay out in the hall waiting. I couldn't see who they were."

"You mean you heard some disembodied voices and you're worrying about what you thought they said? Sara, Sara, you surprise me. Didn't I tell you that this whole thing would be dreamlike, and that you wouldn't remember much of it clearly?"

"I really don't think I was dreaming."

"All right," he humored her. "Then you probably heard somebody talking about someone else. Or you heard wrong. Absolutely wrong, on my honor. I could bring a procession into your room— everybody who was down there today, plus every doctor in this hospital who's had anything to do with your case, and they'd back me up."

"All right. I believe you." She grinned at him. "Don't bring them in—I've had so many doctors in this hospital that the room wouldn't hold them."

"You've passed every test with colors flying. I'm sorry we've had to put you through all this because now the best answer we can come up with is that you had an unidentified virus infection. One that will probably never recur. We can't even take credit for saving your life, but I will certainly feel we've let you down if we can't put your mind at ease."

"If you say not to worry, then I won't worry. I guess I'm pretty lucky."

"I know you're lucky. I only wish all our cases had such happy endings. Just yesterday in staff meeting we decided we had to tell a father he might as well take his young son home to die. His heart has had it—he's had five"—he held up his hand with all fingers spread—"five open-heart operations."

"Is that a lot?"

"Five operations of the sort he's had is practically unheard of. There's not another thing we can do. The father is wealthy—he'd pay anything for a new heart for his son—a new wing for the hospital, anything. He's a desperate man. This is his only child and he can't come to terms with this verdict. I really fear for him as well as for the boy."

Sara shook her head with pity. "It would all but kill my parents if anything happened to me."

"I've sensed that. It was pretty wonderful, I can tell you, to be able to call them a little while ago and tell them that they can relax now, that you've got a long life ahead of you. They're coming to get you day after tomorrow."

"Good." She met his smile with a big one of her own. It got out of control. She turned her brimming eyes away, astonished, embarrassed to be crying again. "I almost never cry."

"I know. But you've been worried, Sara. It's the letdown."

"I've not been too worried, not really." She reached for a paper handkerchief. "But all these weeks I've had nothing much to do except lie here and stare at TV and think about my life. It was kind of a blow to realize that the worst of the daytime serials, even the commercials, were more interesting than my life." She blew her nose and tried to laugh a little. "Twenty-five is kind of old, don't you think, to be having an identity crisis?"

He reached for her hand. "What's wrong with your life?"

"Nothing. I'm a rat to complain. But it's a nothing life in a little town where I will just go on being nothing. It's my own fault, Dr. Durham. I never wanted to—to *be* anything—that's why I didn't finish college." His eyes were so kind, so interested and understanding; she could never have talked to him like this if he had been handsome and young. "I always thought something wonderful was going to—just happen. And then when I had my last birthday all of a sudden it hit me that nobody had come along that I wanted to marry, and I was a quarter of a century old, and I kind of panicked. I knew I ought to do something, but I still don't know what to do. I can see my life going on, year after year, just the same."

"Maybe it needn't." His fingers tightened.

Sara looked away from his face with quick dismay. Oh, no! He was dear and kind, but he was twice her age!

"There now. That slipped out. Forget it for now. A physician gets to know a lot—and not just medically—about a patient who spends as much time in the hospital as you have. I admire you because you are intelligent, brave, and kind. You're resourceful. Take that little hobby of yours, for instance, the contests. I wish more of my patients had something to take their minds off themselves." He started searching through his pockets. "Somewhere here I've got an entry blank one of the fellows down in the lab gave me for you."

Sara was relieved to have the subject changed. "It's more of a habit than a hobby now. I haven't really thought I was going to win anything since I was about twelve, doing puzzles and trying to win a pony. But I seem to go on entering contests sometimes for things I don't even want—like a mink coat. The last thing on earth I want is a coat made out of dead animals."

He found the blank and peered at it. "Well, this one is for a pot of gold, it says here. That might be useful." He put the contest blank on the stack of others. "I've got something else here I want to show you. Some pictures." He got out his bifocals and put them on. "My roses. Now in this one you can see the Peace roses like those on the bureau. This is the little Mirandy that I won a blue ribbon on—I'm proud of that. Tropicana here . . . Souvenir . . ."

The subject, Sara knew, had not been changed. She looked, exclaimed, admired, seeing more than roses against a stone wall. The rambling white house she saw in the background was too big for one man now that his wife was dead and all the children gone; the pool she glimpsed couldn't be much fun to swim in alone.

"I'd like to have you see my place sometime, Sara. My sister is coming to be with me all summer, so if you should think you'd like to come down some weekend—"

"Well, sometime, maybe." She didn't want to hurt him.

When Dr. Durham had left the room she lay there with her blue eyes shadowed. The still look was on her face. Somebody had to win that pot of gold and she supposed that she had as good a chance . . . Forget it. Dr. Durham's implied offer was a lot more realistic. For a bit she tried to visualize herself in that setting, entertaining in that big house, learning the names of the roses. He'd not want children at his age, probably. He would want sex; her mind faltered, but she reminded herself that men his age were supposed to make very satisfactory lovers. She had the thought that she might do worse and it frightened her.

Where was the shaggy-haired young man she had dreamed of, lean of gut, hot-eyed, reaching for her?

Gone. He had never existed.

Fool! screamed The Girl inside her. He would never have looked at sweet Sara Moore.

CHAPTER THREE

Sara lay on her own bed at home in a pretty room with white-painted wicker furniture and blue walls. The hour's ride up from St. Louis had been exhausting with heat waves in shimmering mirages, mile after flat mile. All three of them had sat, as always, in the front seat with Sara in the middle.

Her father was a quiet man with a bony face and dusty brown hair that had not grayed. From time to time he had touched her, grinned at her as if to reassure himself she was really there. Sara's slender, pretty mother, hair still dark with assistance from a bottle, talked all the way home. The Baker twins were having a double wedding in June . . . The Bensons next door were on the verge of divorce . . . Mrs. Holtzhouser, hostess for the last book-club meeting, had inflicted upon the members her daughter Eloise's blurred slides of the Greek isles. Poor Eloise; everybody knew that the reason she took all those trips was to find a man—and she probably would find one; determination paid off. Eloise couldn't wait for Sara to get home. They were the only girls left in the old crowd.

The air conditioner in this room must have been turned on high; Sara's feet were getting cold. The closed windows held close the fragrance of more bouquets, mostly from the gardens of neighbors and friends—irises, peonies, lilacs—artistically arranged or inartistically bunched. Sara could have looked at each bouquet and identified the sender. A jar, not very clean, held dandelions which were trying to close. They were from five-year-old Brenda Jean Benson next door.

From time to time Sara could hear the muffled ring of the telephone. How's Sara? the callers would want to know. She hoped her mother would be able to keep them away for a day or two. Especially Eloise.

When she had said she wanted to lie down for a while, her parents had looked at her with quick concern. No, she was perfectly all right, just a little tired. She had yawned for them, saying she wanted to sleep for a while before dinner. She had not slept; soon she must go downstairs to prove she felt well, show gladness that her life had been restored to her and to them.

She got up, turned off the air conditioner, and opened one of the windows to let in the hot new sweetness of summer. North Maple Street was attractive this time of year with new leaves on the high trees and sprinklers jetting busily on emerald lawns. Flower beds were prim and weedless, and geraniums bloomed in many of the porch boxes. Down the block she saw Miss Flossie climbing her steps one at a time, wearing the same flocked black-and-white voile she had worn for numberless summers.

Across the street Mr. Coovert, a retired farmer, rocked. No geraniums bloomed in his porch boxes; his wife was dead. Every morning in summer he got up and swept the front porch at five o'clock and for most of the day sat there eyeing, quite harmlessly, the women who passed by. Even Miss Flossie.

Except for the Bensons next door, nobody was young on North Maple Street.

Her mother called to say that dinner was ready. They sat together in the dining room, which was used only on special occasions. Sara was touched to see her grandmother's Haviland plates, delicately pastel like the centerpiece of sweet peas.

(In the hospital about now the heavy tray carts would be rattling in the halls. When you lifted the cover on the trays the smell was always the same whether beef, liver, fish, chicken or lamb, a dark smell, promising ptomaine in another smothered hour.)

The chicken breast before her had just been broiled; the peas were from their own garden, as were the radishes, lettuce and onions. Miss Flossie had brought the tender rolls.

Sara had to force herself to eat. Her mother chattered.

A baby shower was being given for Junie Clark next Friday night. Little Junie, why it seemed just yesterday that Sara used to baby-sit with her . . . The Kellerman girl was getting married, and, frankly, Sara's mother was getting sick of hearing about the wedding. "One thing, Sara, when you get married I promise you that I will not wear pastel lace. Honey, you're not eating very much."

"I could get married." Sara's fingers were tight on the goblet stem as she took a sip of iced tea. "Dr. Durham at the hospital. He's a widower, has a beautiful big home—"

"Why, Sara!" Her mother put down her fork. "He's old. Has he actually proposed to you?"

"He's not that old—I think he's around fifty. He hasn't asked me in so many words, but if I take him up on his invitation to come to visit him this summer . . ." She took another sip of tea and lifted her chin. "Lots of older men are attractive. Look at Richard Burton—he's not far from fifty."

With a glance at Sara's flushed face her father said, "Let's go out on the front porch, girl. Mother, you wouldn't mind bringing dessert out there, would you? It ought to be nice there now."

On the vine-shaded front porch the scent of the honeysuckle mingled with the scent of the climbing roses. Sara sat in the big rocker, put back her head and closed her eyes. She could remember rocking in this chair when she was so little her feet stuck straight out in front of her. Her father took the porch swing, not talking for a while. His calm understanding had comforted her all her life.

The porch swing creaked in the well-remembered sound of all the summers of her life in this same town and this same house. After a bit her father said, "Don't settle for second best, Sara. You still look as young and pretty as any of the girls in high school. One of these days the right man will come along. When it hits you, you'll know it. There's plenty of time."

He had said the same words every time any romance had threatened to get serious. Sara had had her share of boyfriends. With two or three of them she might have been happy enough, but honesty forced her to admit to herself that it wasn't her father's comments that had stopped her. She didn't now really regret the loss of any single one of them. The passage of time was something else.

"Actually, we have a pretty good life here, honey, the three of us. Sometimes it takes an experience like the one this family has just gone through to make us realize how lucky we are—agree?"

"Yes," said Sara.

"This September we've got three or four new men coming into the faculty."

Every September Sara met the new men. And every September they got younger.

"We're getting a lot more applications than usual. People are being attracted these days to the peace and quiet of a small town. And Woodsriver really is a pretty good little town."

Sara looked at her father's contented face. He was secure in his job, not ambitious to prove himself further. He knew who he was; she envied him.

"After summer school is over, I've been thinking we ought to take a trip, maybe to the Ozarks. We've still got all that gear, so it wouldn't cost much more than staying at home. We've always had a great time camping, haven't we?"

"Yes," said Sara. "Great."

"Remember how good that fish tasted when we cooked it out in the open?"

She tried to rise to meet her father's enthusiasm. "Remember the time the raccoons got into our food? And the time the baby squirrel fell into Mother's hair?"

"I laugh every time I think of it. Say, sometime we've got to go to Yellowstone. Maybe we can manage it next year."

Sara's mother came out with shortcake, crisp and buttery, with real cream dribbled thickly over the sliced sweetness of the strawberries.

They ate, murmured appreciatively, sipped coffee.

For a bit they talked about what Sara was going to do this summer. Miss Janey's nursery school was always closed for three months. Very few summer jobs were available.

Her mother suggested that she might take the secretarial course the high school was offering this summer. "And then in the fall maybe you'd be equipped to do something besides work at the nursery school."

"I'm no good at office work, Mother. If I have any talent at all it's for working with people."

That reminded Mrs. Moore that there had been a call from the Home yesterday. "Their annual picnic is a couple of weeks away, but they wanted to know if you'd be able to help out."

Sara remembered last year's June picnic. One of the old ladies had wet her pants on the bus and cried. They had sung songs all the way to the lake and back, mostly love songs as there were some elderly courtships under way. The day had been too hot for croquet. She had helped peel down stockings over veined feet, had supported tottering steps as they waded at the edge of the lake like children. Dear, pitiful people; old children.

"I guess so," said Sara.

A lightning bug. Some discussion about whether it was early for lightning bugs. Mr. Coovert's light went out across the street —it must be nine o'clock. Next door their five-year-old neighbor started bawling and they heard Mrs. Benson's shrill "God! What now, Brenda Jean?"

Mrs. Moore said in a low tone that the new minister at the Methodist Church had been counseling the Bensons. "He's one of the new breed. Holds teen rap sessions. The kids like him because he swears and uses their words. Kind of an interesting chap, actually, although I don't pretend to understand the direction the church is taking these days. You've met him, haven't you, Sara? He's got a lot of personality—I mean, looks aren't everything."

Sara stood up abruptly. "I think I'll go to bed and read for a while."

She was lying in bed with a book, not reading, when her mother came in and closed the door. She sat on the edge of the twin bed. "Are you cross with me, Sara?"

"No."

"Your father has been lecturing me. He says I sound as if I am trying to marry you off. Has it sounded that way to you?"

"A little. But I guess every mother wishes . . ."

Her mother said tensely, "Sara, I love you. Your father loves you. It's wonderful having you here with us, but it's wrong. I want you to go someplace. Go to Chicago, Atlanta, any place away from Woodsriver. Move into one of those apartments where they rent just to singles—"

"That's so obvious."

"Maybe it is. I don't know. All I know is that I look into your face and you're not there. In the hospital I thought maybe it was all the medication they had been giving you. Daddy doesn't see it—refuses to admit you're different—so he's no help. I want to help you."

"There's nothing you can do."

"But we've got to think of something—you and I together! Set some sort of realistic goal. And I don't mean those crazy contests you've been entering all your life."

"That. That's over. I tore up the last bunch of entries before I left the hospital."

"Good. And now you've got to *do* something—you've got to *make* something happen!"

"How? Throw myself at some man? I'm just as desperate as Eloise, if you want the truth. The only difference between us is that I've got too much pride to let it show."

They reached for each other's hands and tried to laugh together, but it came off badly. Defenses down, Sara met her mother's eyes. "Listen, I'll tell you something. A couple of days before I left the hospital I overheard two men . . . it sounded like two men . . . whispering about me. One of them said, 'This is the girl. She hasn't a chance.' "

"Sara!"

"Oh, Dr. Durham says I must have dreamed it. He's probably right—I was all doped up—so don't mention it to Daddy. That's not the point anyhow. The point is that I didn't care. I seem to have stopped caring. I don't believe any more that something wonderful is going to happen."

"Oh, my dearest, my very darling." She took Sara into her arms as she had done when she was a little girl.

Sara had saved a few sleeping pills from the hospital. When her mother had gone she took one. After a while, wavelets of sleep began to lap at her consciousness. As the days would lap. The years.

CHAPTER FOUR

The telephone began to ring as soon as Sara came home from the annual picnic at the Home for the Aged.

"Hurry," called her mother who had come out to help unload folding lawn chairs from the station wagon. "That's probably long distance again for you. You had a person-to-person call a little while ago."

But Sara was in the garage putting the croquet set away, and by the time she could get to the phone the ringing had stopped. She thought it might be Dr. Durham; she hadn't written to him yet and she must.

"So how was the picnic?"

Sara was washing her hands now at the kitchen sink. "Oh, the poor old dears all had a wonderful time. I feel good about the way things went."

"I know you do," said her mother.

I know you do, muttered The Girl. She didn't scream much now, although from time to time she called Sara a damned fool.

Maybe I am and maybe I'm not, thought Sara, reaching for a paper towel. There was nothing to be gained by giving in to despair as she had done on that first night at home, and the old groove, for all its dullness, was not unrewarding. The picnic had been a lot of work, but with no real mishaps. One of the old men, hopelessly senile, had kept trying to get his hands on her, but that was nothing new. One of the old ladies who always took out her teeth to eat had lost them. Everybody had clapped when Sara, on her hands and knees in the pine needles, had found them. She was touched by their affection for her, their need.

"Eloise was a real help today. I was glad things went well on her first trial run. She might not be so unhappy if she'd try doing something for somebody else for a change. Does that sound self-righteous?"

"Yes," said her mother. "But all do-gooders get that way eventually. And it's sweet of you to do what you do." She had stopped trying to talk Sara into leaving Woodsriver.

Sara looked up at the planter clock with philodendron trailing over the kitchen sink. "What's for dinner? I know it's early, but I'm starved. We ate at twelve."

"I'm glad your appetite is back. Casserole. I fixed it this morning, and I'll put it into the oven right now so we can eat early. Daddy ought to be along soon. By the way, he said at noon that you can get a job at school when the summer session starts. One of the girls in the office is going to take maternity leave. It's just filing and answering the phone mostly, running errands for him."

"Good," said Sara. "Things seem to be working out." She could start paying back the money her father had lent her to cover the gap between the hospital bill and her major medical insurance.

The phone rang. Sara went into the front hall, got the phone, and trailing the long cord, brought it to the kitchen table. It rang a second time before she picked it up. If Dr. Durham tried to arrange something for a weekend she had decided on a kind, firm no.

The operator said she had a call for Miss Sara Moore.

"Speaking."

A woman's voice came on, not one she had heard before. Sara thought for a moment it was Dr. Durham's secretary. "Is this Miss Sara Moore, 610 North Maple Street, Woodsriver, Illinois?"

"Yes."

"My name is Rita Gomez. I represent the Valley Isle Construction and Finance Company. Congratulations, Miss Moore! I am very happy to tell you that you have just won a trip to the Hawaiian Islands. Fifteen fabulous fun-filled days in our fiftieth state. How does that sound? With five hundred dollars to spend any way you like."

Sara didn't say anything. Her mother was making quiet dinner preparations.

The voice said, "Miss Moore? Can you hear me?"

"Yes, I can hear you." The voice was probably the warmest and most cordial she had ever heard in her life, but it sounded as if it were right here in Woodsriver. She gave a little laugh. "Who is this really?"

"My name is Rita Gomez. I represent the Valley Isle Construction and Finance Company. I was explaining that you have just won—"

"Yes, I heard that part."

There was a chuckle. "It's pretty astonishing news, isn't it? I don't wonder if you can hardly believe it. Can you be ready to leave a week from next Tuesday?"

"A week from next Tuesday? Leave for Hawaii?"

Mrs. Moore collapsed in a chair across from her daughter.

In a daze Sara listened while the friendly voice explained about a prize winner having dropped out at the last minute, and about how June 30 was the end of their fiscal year, making it necessary for the prize expenses to come out of this first six months because they hadn't budgeted any contests for next year. Was that clear?

Sara said she guessed that was clear. Her mother kept murmuring, "Hawaii? *Hawaii?*"

Sara's father walked in and her mother started whispering excitedly.

"Miss Gomez, do I have an option—could I just have the money instead? I happen to owe—"

"I'm sorry, no." Real regret was in her voice. "And we must have your decision. If you are unable to accept, Miss Moore, then of course we'll have to go on to the next person on our list."

"Just a minute—" Sara looked at her parents. "She says she has to have my decision or they'll go on to somebody else."

"Say yes," said her mother.

"Tell her to call you back," said her father.

"Could you call me back, Miss Gomez?"

There was a pause. "I'm calling from Hawaii."

Sara said, "She says she's calling from Hawaii—" and then she covered the phone with her palm. "I think somebody is just putting me on."

Her father got a pen and an envelope from his pocket and put them on the table. "Get her number and tell her you will call her back."

Sara asked for the number, wrote it down, and said she would call back. "Yes, right back, Miss Gomez."

The three of them sat there while Sara repeated everything she could remember. "But I think it's just a gag."

"Why?"

"Well—sort of a hunch, I guess. When I said I would call her I thought she sounded rather taken aback."

"That's natural," said her mother. "Most people would leap at the chance to go to Hawaii without having to think about it twice."

"I guess so. But I could hear her as if she were right here in Woodsriver."

Mr. Moore looked thoughtful. "These days that's how most long-distance calls sound, no matter where they come from. And yet . . ."

It was hot in the kitchen. Sara's face was flushed and her eyes very blue as she looked from one parent to another. "Look—everybody who knows me knows I've entered a lot of contests. It could be somebody with a cracked sense of humor. One of those crazy medics at the hospital could have gotten some nurse to call me. They were always kidding me. Everybody in the whole hospital seemed to know about it."

"Did it sound like any voice you ever heard before?"

She shook her head. "I don't think so. She had a nice voice—terribly friendly. No special accent—but I guess people in Hawaii would sound about like we do." She leaned back, lifting her damp hair off her neck. "Wait a minute. It can't be on the level."

"Why not?"

"Because I have never entered any contest for a trip to Hawaii. Around the world, yes. A hundred dollars a month for life, yes. Record albums, houses, cars. But I am positive that I have never entered any contest for a trip to Hawaii."

Mrs. Moore said, "Sara, be sensible. You have entered so many of these things that you probably just don't remember. Or maybe somebody else sent your name in. Oh, honestly, I can't understand you! You should be hysterical, and here you sit trying to think of reasons why it can't be true!"

"I guess I can't believe it could really be me."

"Why not you? Law of averages. Sara, never look a gift horse—"

Mr. Moore interrupted. "Well, people do win contests. But we must not forget that you were very sick not long ago. I would want to be very sure that Dr. Durham felt there was no likelihood of that virus recurring."

"He has already told us that," said Mrs. Moore with exasperation. She turned to Sara. "Does this remind you of anything—like the time you were getting ready to go to Girl Scout camp and your father got all charged up about poisonous snakes and drownings and you almost didn't go?"

"This is entirely different," he said stiffly.

"It certainly is—she was ten then and now she's twenty-five."

"I am only trying to use some caution. I wonder, for instance, why the big rush? A week from Tuesday is not even two weeks away. Also, aren't the trips people win usually for two? If it were for two your mother could go with you. It sounds kind of funny to me."

"Or phony," agreed Sara.

Mrs. Moore started fanning her face. "I read the other day that all contests have to be on the level now—they're cracking down on the fakes."

"I know, I know, but it's always sensible—" He pushed the envelope and pen closer to Sara. "Why don't you jot down all these things we wonder about so you won't forget to ask them? Then call her back."

She placed the call. After just one ring the same voice answered as if she had been waiting. "This is Miss Gomez."

Sara took a deep breath. So it wasn't just one of her witty friends, and that took care of her first objection. "This is Sara Moore again. I do think there may have been some mistake, Miss Gomez. I

don't remember entering any contest like this. I remember entering one a while back for a trip around the world, but—"

"That was our *first* prize, Miss Moore."

"Oh, I see." She went on to the next question. "Miss Gomez,
trips like this—aren't they usually for two?"

"Our second prize was for two. This is our third prize."

"Oh. Well, here's another thing—the time you have given me
is so short. I've been talking it over with my parents, and that's
what we don't understand." She looked at her mother, who still
sat across the table, hanging on every word, at her father, who had
gone to look out the window.

"Oh. Yes, I can see how that might be a little confusing, although
I did think I had explained it to some extent. All the reservations
were made some time ago, of course, and all the winners duly
notified. Even though our third-prize winner is now unable to
accept, we must, in order to comply with certain regulations, award
each prize as advertised. Does that make everything a little bit
clearer to you?"

"I guess so. Yes, it does."

"Now, if you cannot accept, we shall have to go on to the next
holder of a lucky number, and—"

"*Holder?* But, Miss Gomez, I don't *hold* any lucky number."

That chuckle again across the miles. "Don't worry. Your lucky
number is right here in front of me. Now, if you can accept—"

"Yes, I can accept." She held the phone tightly.

"Oh, very good. That's fine. I'll get a letter of confirmation off
to you right away, explaining everything in more detail. I might
tell you now, since I know you must be pretty interested, that you'll
be staying at first-class hotels on all the islands, beginning with
the Summer Palace Lodge in Honolulu on the island of Oahu. It's
right on the beach, new, and very lovely."

"Summer Palace Lodge," Sara repeated, feeling that she must be dreaming. "Let me write that down."

"Oh, don't bother to write anything down now—you'll have a letter that will give your itinerary in complete detail. You will leave Lambert Municipal Airport in St. Louis sometime around noon on Tuesday, as I recall, and fly to Los Angeles, where there will be a two-hour stopover. From there you will travel first class, of course, by United Airlines on what they call their Red Carpet flight. Your ticket will accompany the letter. When you arrive, I'll meet you and give you your five hundred dollars. Now, Miss Moore, do you have any questions?"

"No, I don't think so."

Mr. Moore said, "Ask her the name of the company again, Sara."

Miss Gomez heard that apparently. "Tell your father that it's the Valley Isle Construction and Finance Company. It's here on the island of Maui, and it's one of several subsidiaries of the Dillingham Corporation. Tell your father that he can easily check on Dillingham if he should feel it's necessary. It's a very old firm, well known, and very highly regarded."

"I'll tell him. Thank you very much, Miss Gomez."

"I shall be looking forward so much to meeting you, Miss Moore. Your plane gets in here around eight, I believe. All right?"

"Yes. Thank you very much."

Sara put the phone back. Her mother gave a little squeal and leaned to grab her. "Oh, I just can't believe it!"

Sara gave a shake to her head. "I can't believe it either." She looked at her father.

"Sure, I guess it's great. I'll check on Dillingham though. And maybe I ought to see if I can find out something about this Miss Gomez."

Mrs. Moore stood up and threw up her hands. "And how about

checking out the Summer Palace Lodge? Maybe it's not fireproof. Also, there must be something you can find out that's wrong with United Airlines!" She jerked the oven door open and leaned to look at the casserole. "*Also,* there's a volcano over there somewhere that erupts."

"Just like at home." He gave his wife a pinch. "Mother, how come we never have any champagne in this house when we need it?"

CHAPTER FIVE

Sara s fatner checked at once on the Dillingham Corporation and found it to be topnotch. The arrival of a letter on heavy Valley Isle Construction and Finance Company letterhead, with the name of Rita Gomez as director of public relations, left him no reason whatever for thinking that the deal was other than it seemed.

The letter started out, "Aloha! Miss Sara Moore," and enclosed her itinerary and her ticket. Happily Sara's mother said she would get a big map of the Islands and keep track of Sara's progress with colored pins.

There was shopping to be done, sewing that somehow had to be managed in the midst of callers who stopped by with bon voyage gifts to talk about Hawaii and marvel at Sara's luck. Adoring little Brenda Jean Benson, a sadly unattractive little girl, complicated everything by being underfoot too many hours out of every day.

She brought Sara a present which she had picked out by herself, jeweled manicure scissors in a glassine box with a dime-store sticker, and insisted on standing by to make sure Sara packed it.

Dr. Durham called to say he had received Sara's letter explaining why she couldn't come for her checkup. He congratulated her on her good fortune; she could come in when she returned. Meanwhile, if she would give him her itinerary, he would consult the American Medical Association Directory and find a good man on each of the islands—not that he expected that she would need a doctor. She received the promised list with a businesslike letter. She was fond of him, grateful for many things, not the least of which was that the letter's tone indicated that he now realized he'd be wise to confine himself to the cordial best wishes of his signature.

She went along with her mother's suggestion that they lighten a few strands of her hair. Trying to put some animation into her voice she said, Yes, she was getting pretty excited now.

Why wasn't it true? Why hadn't she been able to slip into the old way of daydreaming about what might happen, imagining herself meeting some beautiful guy and saying clever lines that would change her life?

Time was that every time her mother sent her to the store she'd had the feeling that something wonderful might wait around the corner. Did good sense finally get its dreary gray net around you when you were a quarter of a century old? She wanted to be thrilled, to let go of inhibitions. Maybe when she got there some magic would take hold, sweep her along into a romantic adventure that would satisfy the hot blood of The Girl and do away forever with the specter of the sweet spinster waiting down the years with blue eyes fading, the dreams all gone.

Maybe. She wished she could believe it.

A few nights before she was scheduled to leave, Sara was awakened by her father's voice making strangled sounds without words. She jumped out of bed thinking he must be struggling with a prowler. But then she heard her mother say, "Hush, dear. Everything is all right. Go back to sleep."

"Go check on Sara. I dreamed about her. Make sure she's all right."

Sara went into her parents' room and saw her father sitting on the edge of the double bed, his head in his hands. "But it was so vivid—I saw it all. I dreamed that she was . . ." He shuddered.

Sara crossed the room and put her hands on his shoulders. "Look, Daddy, I'm perfectly all right."

He looked at her with his nightmare still in his eyes. He said he was sorry and he hoped they could go back to sleep. He was going downstairs to fix himself a drink.

Around ten o'clock the next day, he came home from school sick. Mrs. Moore called the doctor and he stopped by on his lunch hour.

Sara sat with her mother in the living room waiting while the doctor was upstairs. Since midmorning nothing had been accomplished. There were lists half checked off. On the coffee table was a dress that needed hemming. Brenda Jean kept knocking at the back door.

"Don't bother us, Brenda Jean. We're busy."

"But I can see you just sitting there." Brenda Jean picked her nose anxiously, peering through the screen.

"I know, honey, but please go away."

"I'm afraid you'll forget to send me my present."

"How could I?" Sara rolled her eyes. "No, no, I won't forget, honey." She went and closed the back door firmly. Coming back to the living room she said, "If anything is really wrong with Daddy, you know of course that I'm not going."

"Oh, of course." Her mother said it tiredly. She picked up the needle and thread and laid them down again. "I can look down the years, Sara Moore, and see you giving things up."

"But if he's really sick, how could I go? Look at the way he stood by when I was sick—"

Her mother sighed. She picked up the needle and made little short, stabbing sti⸳ches.

"Mother, what was his dream?"

"I don't know. He wouldn't talk about it."

"Something about me—"

"Yes. Oh, sure, about you, Sara. You're going away from him, aren't you?"

"You mean you think that he just—"

"Oh, he had some kind of nightmare, of course. Your father is certainly not a liar, and he did have some kind of dream about you. But I think his dream only reflected his wish to keep you here. I'm no dream expert, but it's clear even to me that dreams are nothing more than the workings of our subconscious minds."

The doctor came downstairs and told them that he had made an examination and there was nothing to worry about. He had known the family all their lives. He would have a prescription sent out.

Sara went upstairs and found her father putting on his shirt. She said, surprised, "What are you getting up for?"

"Because there's nothing wrong with me—Doc told me that in so many words. I'm going back to the office."

"But he's sending a prescription—"

"Too bad. Tranquilizers, probably." He sat down and put on his shoes. "Sara, if I let myself stand in the way of your having this trip I'll never forgive myself. And neither would your mother."

"If I thought you were really sick I wouldn't dream of going

away. Or if I thought that you really, truly did not want me to
go—"

"I know that, girl. You've spoiled me. I don't think you've ever
done anything in your whole life that you thought would worry
me. You're just too damned good."

She gave him a small smile as he stood up. "Good? That's all
you know. Inside I am full of wicked words. Thoughts, desires
you wouldn't believe, Pop."

"Good. Most people, if the truth were known . . ." He gave her
a pat on the cheek. "You go and God bless. Wicked thoughts
and all."

"I wish you would tell me about your dream."

"What dream?" He went past her into the hall. "You just go
to Hawaii."

By the time Sara was ready to board the plane on the following
Tuesday, her father was acting as if he thought the trip was the
greatest idea in the world.

"Live a little," said her mother, holding her close. "Talk to
strangers. But if you should get one of your sore throats, promise
me you'll see a doctor instantly. Write every day."

"She won't have time." Her father hugged her. "G'bye." His
knuckles nudged her chin. "Take it easy, chick. Have the time of
your life."

"What if I meet somebody wonderful and fall in love?"

"I hope you do."

"What will you do if he lives in Australia?"

"Follow you. They need teachers there, I hear. But I promise
that your mother and I won't live next door." He gave her a big
kiss and a little spank to hurry her through the door. When she
turned to look back he held up a circled thumb and finger. Her
mother was waving and blowing kisses and crying a little.

CHAPTER SIX

The lights of Honolulu looked like jewels, boxed and crammed in the center of the darkness. More jewel-like strands were flung, draped, looped and spilled all over Oahu, second largest of the Hawaiian Islands. Sara put the travel book that Eloise had given her into her shoulder bag. She had memorized a few words. She was a *haole,* meaning a white person, and pronounced howly; also, she was a *wahine,* girl; *mahalo* was the word for thank you; *pau,* pronounced pow, meant finished.

She doubted if she'd ever have the nerve to go past *aloha.*

The small gold watch her parents had given her said it was a little past midnight. She turned it back four hours and stood up when the plane came to a stop. Most of the other first-class passengers were convention-bound. Some of them already wore aloha shirts and muumuus, and a few by now were joyously drunk.

Sara had had only one Mai Tai, but she felt punchy as she deplaned to the loud strains of "Blue Hawaii." The passengers were scanned for identifying badges, and the conventioneers were automatically lassoed with leis. She stood alone. It was a little like the time at a magic show when she had been singled out of an audience of tots and lifted to the stage and set down, lights glaring, not quite knowing what she was doing there.

An exotic girl with upswept black hair was striding toward her. For one bemused moment Sara thought she looked like the magician's helper who had dazzled her on that long-ago occasion. A few years older than Sara, she had the assurance of the very beautiful. She spoke in the voice that Sara remembered from the phone.

"I'm Rita Gomez, and you must be Sara Moore. Aloha! Welcome to Hawaii!" She settled a lei of white flowers around Sara's shoulders and leaned to give her the kiss of aloha—proper, Sara had read, when presenting a lei. "How pretty you are! What a sweet little dress. Did you have a good flight?"

"Perfect. I haven't quite got my feet on the ground yet." She inhaled the fragrance of the flowers. "Thank you, Miss Gomez."

"Rita, of course." She gave Sara's arm a little squeeze. "I'm sure we're going to be great friends. We go this way to get your luggage. Just give me your claim check. I've rented a car."

Rita drove the white Toyota expertly, talking smoothly. The unreality persisted as the many-syllabled street signs flashed by. Now they had left the industrial section behind and Sara began to see flowering trees standing tall and unbelievable, like bouquets for a race of giants.

The Summer Palace Lodge was unbelievable too. Torches flamed outside a low Polynesian structure with wings rising to the rear and curving back around a large swimming pool. In the lobby brilliant birds flew from branch to branch in a jungle setting, seemingly confined only by the jets of a fountain that reached from floor to roof.

Her room was like something out of a movie about the very rich. A gold shag rug covered the floor, and on the vast circular bed was a splashy gold-and-white spread. Matching draperies came to the floor, and beyond them she saw a balcony overlooking the pool below. She had to touch the flowers in a big bouquet on the chest to make sure they were real.

Even the money which Rita gave her seemed like play money. Rita said she wanted her to count it, and the bills were so flat and new she had to count them twice. Under Rita's gaze she felt like one of the nursery kids trying to remember what came after four. "I can't quite seem to come down to earth yet, but I guess the five hundred is all here. My father suggested that I put it into traveler's checks."

"Good idea, sweetie. Maybe I can take you to a bank tomorrow. It's all yours to lose or blow or save, you know. I'll be paying all your regular expenses."

Rita lit a cigarette. They were sitting together on a small sofa by the coffee table. "And now I think we'd better have a little talk. There are a couple of things I had better explain to you so there won't be any misunderstandings that might cause hard feelings. I am going to be very strict. You will probably think I am like a bossy big sister." She smiled brilliantly.

Sara's own smile felt uncertain. There was something about all this smooth self-assurance that put her off a bit.

"You see, sweetie, I am completely responsible for you. So I shall have to ask you not to go anywhere at all without me. Is that clear?"

The words were clear enough. There seemed to be a condescension behind them which her next words did nothing to dispel.

"You are young and pretty and"—she gave an amused little laugh—"I don't know how innocent you are, but you do give that impression. Oh, don't get me wrong, it's charming, but Honolulu is just full of people who might take advantage of you."

Sara was annoyed to realize that color had come into her cheeks. The few words she had said in the last hour had not, perhaps, been brilliant. She wished she could get rid of the feeling that this whole thing was some sort of performance on a set that would be struck when the curtains fell revealing bare emptiness. She wished Rita were not quite so much like an actress who knew all her lines, instructing a rather stupid stand-in who didn't know what the play was all about.

Rita gave a hasty pat to her knee. "All I'm saying is that my boss over on Maui trusts me to look after you, and I certainly wouldn't want anything to happen to jeopardize my new job."

"How long have you had it?"

"Just a few weeks. I was working here in Honolulu when I answered an ad. Out of all the girls who answered, I seemed to have the qualifications they were looking for. A marvelous break. Now, let's talk about what you would like to see tomorrow. I notice you have what looks like a guidebook sticking out of your bag over there. I'm sure you've been reading up."

Sara tried to put her feeling of annoyance behind her. After all, Rita would probably have to be somewhat officious to have this job. "I'd like to go to Sea Life Park and the Polynesian Cultural Center. That museum that's supposed to be a must, and—"

"Bishop Museum. Yes, everybody ought to see that. I thought we might go there tomorrow afternoon. We'll not have time enough to see everything on this island, of course. According to our schedule, we'll be leaving for Maui on Friday. It so happens that in the morning I will be pretty well tied up. Something has come up that my boss wants me to take care of. But I'm sure you'll want to rest then, anyhow."

"I doubt that." Sara said it coolly as she got up and went over to the mirror and looked past the extravagance of flowers. Her appearance reassured her. She was glad her mother had insisted that she do something to her hair; the effect gave her a little kick every time she looked into the mirror. She did look young. She was glad of that. She did look pretty. And if this trip didn't make a difference in her life, she deserved whatever might wait for her in Woodsriver.

"Remember what I told you about being bossy—" In the mirror she saw Rita wag a finger at her. "I happen to know what this time change does to people and I don't want you collapsing on me. You must get at least eight hours of sleep. It is now, according to your time, past one o'clock. A lazy morning will do you good. When you wake up, call room service and have your breakfast sent up. Try the fresh pineapple—all the tourists have a fit over it. Maybe then you would like to lie in the sun on your balcony for a few minutes."

"I'll probably go down to the pool after breakfast."

"Oh, no, sweetie. This tropical sun does terrible things to people. You just take fifteen minutes or so out on that balcony—that's plenty for the first day. Did you bring sun lotion?"

"Of course. Don't worry about me."

Rita went to pull the draperies shut so the sun wouldn't bother her in the morning. "Well, you do as I say, Sara, and we'll get along just fine. I intend to take very good care of you. I'm sure your parents must have worried a little, having you go off like this."

"Oh, I think they trust me to have sense enough to look out for myself."

"Good for them." Smile met smile. "You just tell them when you write that I am going to be just like a duenna. That's what you can do in the morning, write cards and letters." She opened the middle drawer of the desk. "Yes, there are plenty of postcards and stationery in here. Need any help with unpacking?"

"No, thanks." She just wished Rita would go.

"Nighty night, then. I'll be right next door. Sleep late in the morning and I'll see you around noon."

Sara unpacked and got ready for bed. The bathroom was all pale marble and gold, with faucets shaped like mermaids. Frosted bulbs surrounded her mirror, giving a flattering light. She cleansed her face and wondered how long it would be before a good tan merged her freckles.

At home it would soon be time for another day to begin, but she did not feel sleepy when she got into bed. The feeling of un-reality still lingered and she rather liked it. In spite of the rules laid down by her new duenna she intended to do just as she pleased until noon tomorrow.

The big round bed gave her a freedom no single bed had ever given her. She flung her arms wide and smiled into the dark.

The strands of the dreary gray net of common sense began to loosen. A fantasy or two began to take place, not sensible. She talked herself to sleep with words that were witty, daring.

CHAPTER SEVEN

Sara woke with a feeling of anticipation as unaccustomed as the fragrance of her white-ginger lei that hung, only a little faded, across one corner of the mirror. She put her bare feet into the thick shag of the carpet. Golden light was coming in around the edge of the draperies that Rita had pulled shut the night before.

She opened the draperies wide, turned off the air conditioning, and slid back the glass door. The air moved a little in contrast to the still coolness of her room. It was silky warm, not hot, just right.

Below her was the pool shaped, as promised in the brochure, like the island of Oahu. A tiny brown man with a pointed stick was picking up blossoms that had fallen on the brown mulch and putting them into a bag over his shoulder. He looked up and saw her and smiled. She smiled back.

A glance at her watch told her it was just a little past nine, so the morning hadn't been wasted after all.

"Aloha!" said a voice when she picked up the telephone. "Aloha!" She slid into the friendly greeting with an ease that surprised her. She ordered a lavish breakfast, and Room Service promised to send a tray right up.

Rita was right about the pineapple.

After breakfast, Sara got out the postcards and started in on them, knowing she was never going to stop long enough to bother with them once this day got under way. On every card except the one to her parents, she copied a few Hawaiian words that meant "Having wonderful time. Wish you were here." It fit with her somewhat skittish mood not to translate. The truth was that she didn't wish any of them were here. Certainly not Eloise. And not Dr. Durham, she thought as she addressed one of the cards to him at the hospital.

She ruined the first card she wrote to her parents. After a few adjectives about how wonderful it all was she had said, "But I can't say that I like Rita Gomez very much." She looked at the words and then tore up the card, knowing it might worry them if they thought everything wasn't one hundred percent perfect. She wrote another, leaving in the adjectives and adding, "Rita Gomez tells me she is going to be very strict with me. I may feel as if I am traveling with my grandmother!"

A swimming class seemed to be in progress down in the pool, so that was out for now. She put on a yellow dress, some new yellow sandals, and walked out into the yellow sunshine with a delicious breeze lifting her hair.

Before she had gone a block she realized that she had left the postcards on the table beside her door, and that she had forgotten to ask the desk clerk about a bank. It didn't matter; she could mail the cards later and probably she would come to a bank. It was good having this one morning to herself to walk along the wide, clean streets, stopping when she felt like it, smiling at happy-looking people who, in Rita's words, might take advantage of her.

In the window of a small Japanese shop, a man flipped a knife quickly, opening oysters and finding pearls. Sara went inside to watch. The oysters were also available in cans with pearls guaranteed. She bought one and had it sent to Brenda Jean, hoping the child wouldn't lose the pearl instantly and drive her poor mother crazier than she seemed to be already.

The prices in an elegant store further on shocked her, but she bought a muumuu for her mother and finally found an aloha shirt she thought her father might wear. He might be the laughingstock of Rotary, but the high school kids would love it. With no idea of buying it, she tried on a modified *holoku*.

"This is our angel-back," said the almond-eyed clerk with soft persuasion. "See how graceful it is when you walk? See how it clings to your pretty bosom? Feel that silk. Oh, that blue with your eyes, miss, and that yellow with your hair . . ."

Sara bought it. The money in her billfold reminded her that she must try now to find a bank. The clerk gave her directions and it seemed that she followed them, but the names of the streets confused her. By the time she found the bank and came out again she realized that she was lost. She wandered, though happily enough, with no idea where the Summer Palace Lodge might be.

In the International Market Place an international hodgepodge of people surged about her: women tourists in big hats with sunburned arms and bags with shells spelling out Hawaii spoke with accents that could have come from Woodsriver; kids who could have come from colleges anywhere wandered, barefoot and long-haired, with apparent aimlessness through the maze of shops; a band of young men with shaved heads and saffron robes chanted and passed out tracts; a stately group in the native garb of some African nation conversed with an Oxford accent among themselves.

Most of all, Sara was charmed by the golden look of so many of the faces. She didn't know what racial strains produced such a look, but she did know that she was suddenly bored with her own Caucasian skin and pale hair and eyes. There wasn't much she could do about changing her own coloring, but did she have to pass on, unenlivened, such dull, Anglo-Saxon purity to her children?

She chose a father for her children. He sat alone sipping a drink in a shadowed bar where discordant instruments twanged softly. With his white turban held by a large jewel he could have been a prince of some Indian state. His nose was high and arrogant, his black beard neatly trimmed, and his eyes twinkled when they looked at her as if he might be thinking of adding her to his harem.

Sara walked on. A realistic thought intruded: he was more likely a seller of cheap jewelry at one of the Market Place stalls. But she wished she had Eloise's nerve; if she had returned that smile she might have had the chance to talk to him for a while. Nobody looked like that in Woodsriver.

It was late. Hurriedly she asked directions to the Summer Palace Lodge. When she reached it Rita was standing outside waiting for her.

"Where have you been?" She wore her bright smile, but the fingers that closed over Sara's arm were tight.

"Oh—shopping. And I went to a bank and got the traveler's checks."

"I have been terribly worried about you. Nobody at the desk had any idea where you had gone."

"Oh, Rita, be reasonable. What could happen in broad daylight?"

"What could happen to a girl alone in a big city? Don't you read the papers? Sweetie, you could have been robbed, raped, God knows what. You could have been knocked down and killed by one of these wild Honolulu drivers."

Sara turned abruptly, annoyed at being treated like a disobedient child. Over her shoulder she said, "I'm going up to take a shower."

Rita followed her. "Why are you limping like that?"

"I think I have blisters on my heels."

Upstairs they went into their separate rooms. Almost at once, Rita tapped on Sara's door. "Here are a couple of Band-Aids—I thought you might not have any." She smiled at Sara, nicely now. "You think I'm an awful worry-wart, don't you?"

"Well—yes. But thanks for the Band-Aids."

Rita picked up the pile of postcards that lay on the table. "I'll go on down to the lobby and mail these for you. You get your shower as soon as you can and I'll meet you down there. We might as well have lunch here before we go sightseeing."

The room was chilled. The maid who had come in to do up the room must have turned on the air conditioning. Sara turned it off and opened the glass doors as she had done this morning. Several persons were in the pool. Left to her own devices, she would have put on her new bikini and gone down for a dip right now. A very attractive man, blond with a deep tan, sat alone with a drink at one of the little tables.

As she turned from the balcony, she saw Rita. She was standing beside a trash container, tearing something into small pieces. It looked to Sara like one of her postcards. Rita pushed the scraps into the container and strolled toward the lobby.

Perplexed, angry, Sara took a shower, dropping the soap twice and getting her hair wetter each time she retrieved it. Which card had Rita torn up? And why? This was only the beginning of her fifteen fabulous days, but they weren't going to be very fabulous if she didn't give Rita Gomez a piece of her mind.

Sara said nothing until they were seated at the luncheon table and had given their orders. The words, all planned in the shower, came out easily enough.

"In the few hours that I have known you, you have cautioned me about getting enough sleep, not getting too much sun, being robbed, raped, and I don't know what all. I know you are responsible for me, but does that include censoring my mail?"

Rita's dark eyes widened. "I haven't the slightest idea what you are talking about."

"I saw you tear up one of my postcards and put it into the trash container."

Rita reached for a cigarette. She laughed a little. "Now, why would I do a thing like that?"

"I can't imagine. But I saw you. I was looking down from my balcony, and I very plainly saw you tear up one of my cards and stuff it into that trash thing."

Rita put her hand over Sara's. "Oh, Sara, you're a funny little thing. Really you are. I did tear something up, but it was only a tour-bus schedule I had picked up earlier at the desk when I was so worried about where you had gone."

Sara didn't say anything.

"From that distance it could, I suppose, have looked like one of your postcards." She cocked her head. "Maybe those wide, pretty blue eyes need glasses?"

"Twenty-twenty."

Rita touched her hand again. "You and I have gotten off to sort of a bad start, haven't we? It makes me feel sad. It's all my fault, I suppose. But I'm new at this job, and I'm trying awfully hard to be conscientious."

Their food came. They ate. Rita talked charmingly, obviously trying to put Sara's doubts at rest.

But Sara was conscious of a hovering uneasiness all during their tour of the Bishop Museum that afternoon. She tried to take in the represented history of the Hawaiian people who, less than two hundred years before, had lived in a Stone Age culture. She looked at a grass shack and the tools and implements used in the daily life of the lowliest *kanaka.* She gazed at the possessions of the *alii,* the thrones, the jewelry, an enormous feather cloak mostly yellow with red and black geometrical designs. Half a million tiny feathers and generations of painstaking work had been required to complete this priceless relic.

It would have been a lot to take in all at once even if she had been able to give her mind to it completely, to shake off the feeling that Rita's glib explanation had been a lie.

But what was one postcard of no intrinsic value? Sara had managed to throw off the nagging worry about it by the time they reached Sea Life Park. Thousands of fish, striped, colored like flowers, patterned like butterflies, swam beyond the big curving walls of glass underground. In the open air they watched a show where trained dolphins and whales leaped, barked and retrieved.

Dinner was another change of pace that night at La Ronde, a restaurant that revolved once an hour high above the bright lights of Honolulu. When they got up to leave it was only nine o'clock, but Rita said, "You'll be glad, I know, to turn in early tonight."

"Oh, no," Sara said with dismay. "I could go on for hours. Let's. I read about some very interesting-sounding places in that little magazine they gave us at the Lodge."

"They're tourist traps, sweetie. Bunches of men on the prowl, all looking for just one thing. And two girls alone, as if they're hoping to be picked up? No, no, I'm not like that and I'm sure you're not either." Her voice was too firm for argument.

Back in her room, Sara wrote to her parents, telling them about her day. She rambled on for pages, since there was nothing else to do. "Rita Gomez is determined that nothing shall happen to me. Here I am tucked in bed, so to speak, at nine-thirty, with all that glamorous night life going on without me . . ."

She finished her letter and went out to sit on the little balcony for a while. A palm tree made lemon slices of the tropical moon. Inside the Lodge, guitars moaned sweetly with a sound she had come all this way to hear. A voice sang "Beyond the Reef," and she listened to words about the sea, dark and cold, and dreams growing old. On the paths below, couples strolled in the scented night, their arms about each other. Nobody else was all alone.

From Rita's room, a voice. Wasn't Rita alone?

Sara put back her head to listen. Apparently she was just talking on the phone. "Darling, darling, I know. All this wonderful wickedness all around me and here I am, in my bed alone." Soft laughter. "Of course I'm all alone, you bastard. True to you and you know it. You may not have known me long, but you know me well. *Very* well . . ."

A pause and then, "No problem. I did what you told me to do this morning and they think it will be ready day after tomorrow . . . Well, they had to put that special fitting on—oh, the *thing,* the valve, or whatever you call it . . . Love, don't be cross. I don't pretend to know anything about it—that's your department . . . My department? Listen, I told her that the reason we had to turn in early was because Honolulu wasn't safe for two innocent young girls—she believes everything I tell her. Oh, I'm earning my money . . . Right, I'll take good care . . . See you Friday, darling. M-m-mh!"

For a few moments Sara sat very still. And then she hurried from the terrace into her room. She hummed the song she had just heard, but her dreams had by no means grown old. Not yet. She got out the blue-and-gold dress and put it on, turning to see the graceful angel back, glad for the provocative fit over her high round breasts. She pulled her hair up and let it cascade a little carelessly down the back. She'd get a flower, a gold something from the big bouquet out there. A bit of blue-gray shadow for her eyes and some glosser for her lips. She needed no color for her cheeks; they were pink with her anger.

She broke the cellophane on a bon-voyage bottle of perfume, sprayed it furiously, and was ready to go.

CHAPTER EIGHT

Sara hurried past the pool, entered the lobby with its jungle of bright birds and jetting water, moved slowly into the bar and sat at a small table.

Now she was nervous. Never in her life had she done a thing like this. Should she act as if she expected someone? Look at her watch, frown a little, lean to look past the massed plantings? Or just sit here, pretending to be brass-bold, returning the look of a man who leaned on the long curving bar and stared at her, drink in hand?

No. He was glassy-eyed. She let her gaze slide past several pairs of eyes. The man she had seen at the pool this noon was at the other end of the bar talking to some other men. She met his look for a moment and then dropped her eyes to the table, bare except for an ashtray.

She wished now that she hadn't stopped smoking. A cigarette

gave you something to do. You could take your time about light-
ing it, inhale thoughtfully, pick a crumb of tobacco from your lip,
blow out smoke and watch it as if you wondered where it would
go. You could tap the ash, study the glowing tip, gesture with it,
hang on for a kind of safety that could at times seem lifesaving
even though courting—if the Surgeon General was right—an earlier death.

The blond, tanned man was coming toward her from the other
end of the bar. She had nothing to hang on to. Nobody had even
come to take her order for a drink yet. She wound her watch so
tight that she feared for the mainspring.

"Hi. We met at Roz What's-her-name's party. Mind if I sit
down?"

"Oh, hi. Sit down." Easy enough.

"I'm lousy at names. Joe Egan. And you're—?"

She told him. Their eyes met, sizing each other up, smiling a
little.

She put her elbows on the table and leaned on her folded hands,
feeling pretty. She said, "There were so many people that night.
A yacht is no place to remember names. How's Roz these days?"

"Got married."

"To the Black?"

"The brain surgeon? No. His mother is a frightful snob. I
heard Roz married an older man. Member of the Supreme Court,
seems somebody said."

These were lines she had never rehearsed, but she moved into
them easily, meeting the glint in his eyes with a gaze that was
wide and sober. "But Roz was old—ninety-three. The last time
she had her face lifted she couldn't shut her eyes."

He let out a yell of laughter. "You win. Oh, I'm glad you picked
me up—"

"I picked—?"

"Hush. You did. You gave me a signal I never miss. Shall we order something here or go someplace else?"

They walked down the street to a place that looked like a huge grass shack. Dozens of tables surrounded a pit where a flaming sword dance was in progress. Sara ordered a drink that came in a hollowed-out pineapple with fruits floating, and he ordered bourbon on the rocks.

A hula was on the stage now. The rotation of the girls' navels was astonishing. "Keep your eyes on their *hands,*" the master of ceremonies kept saying. Men in the audience stamped on the floor and growled like dogs as one spotlighted girl tossed off her grass skirt and leaned back in an orgiastic ecstasy to the mounting frenzy of the drums.

"Had enough?" said Joe. "Finish that garbagey-looking drink —no, no, love, don't keep the orchid, tourists do that—and I'll take you to another place I know. The Eagle's Nest at the Cavalier. People who really know this town go there. You won't see many tourists. No floor show. No grass-shack music."

They waited out on the street for a taxi. Sara read more than casual friendliness in his eyes. It underscored their exchange of information. He was a sales representative from California, came here several times a year on business. She told him about the contest.

"So people really win those things. And they turn their pretty winners—for which, praise God—loose on the town?"

Sara explained about Rita Gomez. He said to hell with Rita— right? Right.

The Cavalier Restaurant was almost downtown. A doorman opened doors that led through a carved façade. Paintings on the walls made it seem almost like an art gallery. Upstairs, the Nest had the intimacy of a club, quiet in spite of all the people. They sat with padded leather curving high about them. Somewhere a girl singer murmured a soft smoky song into a mike; you didn't have to listen.

Sara sipped at the specialty of the house, which had no floating garbage. Joe finished his bourbon quickly and ordered another. They nibbled at snacks which he said were called *pupus*. They talked, laughed a little softly. His compliments were deft, more bold now, and his plans for the ending were plain.

She said, "Uh—Joe, hold just a minute. Somewhere along the way you've picked up the wrong idea."

"I don't think so. From the minute I saw you sitting there in that bar—"

"That was a mistake, the bar."

He shrugged. "Bar, church, whatever. You can't fool an old pro. I looked at you and I knew."

"Knew what?"

"That you're my favorite type. I love all you wide-eyed demure little girls who sit with your skirts pulled down and your knees together like Mama said. But made for lovin' and you know it. Am I very far wrong?"

No, she thought. Regretfully she said, "Joe, I've not been fair. This is fun and I like you a lot, but—"

He touched the flower in her hair. "Worn on the right means a girl is available—"

She put one finger to his left hand where a circle showed a little lighter than the tan. "How come the good ones are always gone? You're married, of course."

"Don't change the subject. To a very permissive wife. Great gal. She understands me. We've got a great marriage."

"Kids?"

"Two. Boy and girl. Great kids. But none of that has anything to do with any of this."

"Do you always look for a girl?"

"Always. When I was a kid I played kid games. You said you were twenty-five, so let's dispense with the protests and go on back. I've got a bottle in my room."

"Do I look like a first-nighter?" She smiled when she said it.

He considered. "I hate labels. What do you want me to say?"

"Once in every girl's life she needs to think she looks like a threat to decent women."

"Oh, hell, you're working up to no."

"But I'll never forget that once in Honolulu ... Let's go."

At her door he said, "Are you sure this is all you need to remember about Honolulu?"

"It's been frabjous."

"Callooh, callay. Sara, look, I don't have to leave tomorrow. I still know some things about you that you're denying. I can easily arrange to stay on for another twenty-four hours and then you wouldn't be a first-nighter."

Sara stood on tiptoe and kissed his cheek. "Give my love to Roz What's-her-name."

She shut the door. In the marble bathroom she sat before the dressing table and took the faded flower from her hair. *Pop, listen ...*

Would her father understand when she told him about Joe Egan? She knew he would.

So there I was that night, Pop, mad at Rita and sick of being a good little tourist. I didn't want to go to bed at ten o'clock clutching my guidebook, and so ...

She could imagine the way his boyish face would look while he listened, laughing a little, agreeing that it must have been fun. *But what about Joe Egan? Weren't you aware that when a girl lets a man pick her up in a bar he expects to end up in bed?*

Sara started taking down her hair. *So once he got fooled, Pop.*

§ *59*

Do the Joe Egans of this world really deserve to have one hundred percent success?

Don't beg the question, girl. You did a crazy thing and you got away with it. But the thing is . . .

Sara cut off the sound of her father's voice. The thing is, it was fun. She went to bed.

CHAPTER NINE

Sara decided the next day that it didn't make much difference whether or not she liked Rita Gomez. Nor was she going to let herself be bothered by what she had overheard Rita say about her. It pleased her to think she had been smart enough to get out from under Rita's thumb one night for what she realized was a somewhat unwise little adventure.

But she didn't regret it; it was a meager enough little escapade to hug to her breast when she got back to Woodsriver. She didn't regret limiting it either; casual coupling wasn't for her.

Rita was all bright-eyed charm today, putting herself out to be informative. They drove north and saw the stunning view from the wind-swept Pali, the cliff where King Kamehameha had pushed the enemy warriors over the edge to their deaths. They followed the highway that bore his name up along windward

Oahu. There were no billboards. The travel posters Sara had not quite believed now seemed an understatement.

On the *mauka* side, away from the sea, rose the jagged green razorback mountains; on the *makai* side, where dark lava cascaded down into the water, the ocean was cobalt, aquamarine and purple over the coral. Far out on the distant crests the bronze bodies of surfers rose high on their boards, fell, paddled back to try their skills again.

They stopped to buy palm-leaf hats for fifty cents from a charming little lady at a thatched lean-to beside the ocean. A little further along, caged mynah birds called hoarse alohas when they stopped for lunch. The place was called Pat's and Sara was grateful for a name she could pronounce.

They spent two hours at the Polynesian Cultural Center touring a miniature world of the Pacific Islands where students from the nearby college explained their native cultures. She took pictures of the white Mormon Temple (the "Taj Mahal of Hawaii"), the Sacred Falls of Kaliuwaa, and one of a sign to prove there really was a town spelled Kaaawa.

On their way back they detoured through miles of hibiscus hedges to pass beautiful homes under shower trees that spilled long panicles of blossoms, golden and rainbow-hued. Poincianas were everywhere, like umbrellas on fire.

Sara also added a little to her knowledge about Rita that day. Some of it Rita told her. Gomez was a Portuguese name, but she had a mingling of blood that included Oriental and some Hawaiian. She had been born on Maui and had lived there until a year and a half ago.

By observation, Sara learned more about her at the end of the day when they went through the Ala Moana shopping center. Casually Rita removed her inexpensive watch to try on one studded with diamonds. With a calm flip of prohibitive price tags, she tried on dresses, murmuring questions about packability. A trip, thought Sara, wondering if it might be to South America since she had seen travel brochures for that country in the car. She was probably having an affair with the boss, judging by the words overheard last night. It was moderately interesting.

When they got in the car Sara said, trying to assimilate some of this new information, "You're ambitious, aren't you?"

"What are you getting at?"

"You have a goal. I admire people who know what they want out of life and go after it. I've never really known how I should—"

Rita interrupted. "Right now what I want out of life is to get through this traffic without getting crushed."

That could mean Shut up, thought Sara, and she did so. She also wanted safe passage through traffic where there were few lights and every driver seemed to be on his own. But she was realizing that Rita had a way of turning her off every time the conversation got personal.

All afternoon during the sightseeing, Rita had reminded her of the sort of teacher who stands before her class brilliantly informative but with no personal interest in her pupils. She was only three or four years older than Sara, but she had never asked her any of the usual questions about boyfriends or her home life or her ambitions.

Perhaps Rita had a bit of contempt for the dreamy, impractical people who entered the contests put on by her company. Since prizewinners were her job, she would steer them efficiently through the sights and take good care of them but she would draw a sigh of relief when she was through with them. Sara had a feeling that to Rita she would eventually be just one of many names in a file folder.

And then after they got back to the Summer Palace Lodge, Rita said something that made her seem, for the moment, almost warm and human. "I've just been thinking, Sara. Why don't you put in a call to your parents?"

"Are you serious?" It hadn't occurred to her that she would call them all the time she was away.

"Sure. Why not? You've had a wonderful day, haven't you? So why not pick up the phone and tell them all about it while it's fresh in your mind?"

Sara looked at her watch. It was six o'clock. That meant it would be ten at home. Both her parents would almost surely be there. They would not have gone to bed yet. She looked into Rita's smiling face. "It would cost an awful lot—I mean, I could never keep it down to three minutes—"

"So? What's money? Mr. Nielsen has millions."

"Is he the boss?"

"Yes. And very generous."

Her idea of Rita's ambitions were revised upward.

"The call will just go on the bill—no problem. Want me to place it for you?"

"Oh, no. I'll do it." Sara wished that Rita would go on to her own room, but she only went out to sit on the balcony.

Sara made herself comfortable on the bed. It was no time at all before she heard the phone at home begin to ring. She smiled visualizing the scene. They would probably be sitting in the creaking porch swing. They might be talking about her and wondering how she was getting along. The creaking would stop. *Was that the phone? Now, who's calling at this time of night?*

"Hello?" It was her mother's voice.

"Aloha! Guess who this is. Me, Sara."

"Sara! What's wrong?"

"Nothing's wrong. Everything is absolutely wonderful. I just thought I'd call you."

"Wait a minute. Let me move this phone out to the kitchen and shut the door. I've got TV going in the living room."

Sara could see that kitchen just as plainly as if she were there. The round kitchen table where her mother would put the phone. The philodendron trained to run along the top of the windows over the sink.

"There, now." Her mother sounded breathless. "Oh, it's so exciting to hear from you. Daddy should be home any minute—he's at a meeting. He's fine and I'm fine, but tell me how you are and all about every single thing."

"I'll never be able to—you'd never believe it. You should see this bed—it's round. You should see the hibiscus hedges. And the philodendron grows so high in the trees it makes your neck hurt. Today we went—but I'll write you. I just love the people here, and the climate and the flowers and the food—"

"Oh, Sara, Sara, you sound so different—just like the way you used to be—"

"That's how I'm beginning to feel. What's new in Woodsriver?"

"Well, Mr. Coovert had a date with Miss Flossie. She's been bringing him pies and rolls all spring, but nobody dreamed—! Today I heard that the Bensons would get a divorce but neither of them wants custody of Brenda Jean."

"Ah, that poor kid. Tell her I sent her present."

"Honey, I've got a great big map of all the Islands right in front of me here on the kitchen wall with colored pins stuck in it. Tomorrow you're going on to the Aloha Nui on Maui. I've already sent one letter there. And remember when you come back I want you to speak to my book club."

Sara groaned.

"Get some little human-interest things to tell, honey. Get a few laughs. Wait, I think I hear your father driving into the garage—"

"Before he comes, tell me one thing. Did he ever tell you anything about that dream he had?"

"Oh, that. It really was the silliest thing. It was about the hospital, of all things. I mean, why worry about the past? Here's your father—"

"Hello, Sassie."

"Hello, darlin'—" He hadn't called her Sassie since she was four years old.

"Are you all right? Your voice doesn't sound quite—"

"Of course I'm all right." She reached for a tissue and blew her nose. "If you must have the truth, I'm crying a little—I mean, I'm just so glad to hear your voice, and everything is so marvelous, and . . . listen, you and Mother have got to start saving because I wouldn't be a bit surprised if I just stayed here—some of these Island people are pretty exciting, Pop. They look like prototypes of a future race."

He was laughing. "You sound to me as if you've had about three martinis."

"No, but I saw a guy yesterday—he looked like a prince, or something. Indian, maybe. I mean, do you have any set ideas of what your grandchildren must look like?"

"No, I don't. We'll probably move right down the street so we can spoil 'em. But take it easy, chick."

"I will. Daddy, you aren't worried any more about me, are you?"

"Who, me?"

"Oh, you are one crazy fella."

Rita was coming into the room.

"I've got to go now. This phone call must be costing an awful lot."

"I know. Take care of your dear self, Sassie."

"I will, I will. You too. Aloha, Daddy."

"I thought that meant hello—"

"It does. And it means I love you. But aloha also means goodbye."

CHAPTER TEN

On the way to the airport the next morning they made a stop downtown to pick up a large package, bread-box size, which Rita said was a piece of equipment for her boss's jet.

"Jet?" Sara revised her idea of Rita's ambitions upward again.

"Oh, sure. He keeps it there in case they should decide to buzz off to one of their other homes. They have a place in Maine. Another in Phoenix—'da kine' money, as we say in the Islands."

Rita held the box on her lap during the half-hour flight to the Kahului airport on Maui. When they got there she asked Sara to wait while she delivered the package; apparently it was important.

There was no rental car this time. Rita slid under the wheel of a white Mercedes which was waiting for them, and explained as she took a key from her purse that this would be theirs to use on this island. The boss had other cars, of course.

Maui was a country island with plantations of sugar cane and fields of low-growing pineapple that looked like random patch-work of blue-green corduroy on the slopes between the mountains and the sea. No freeways; no big cities. They drove south through towns with exotic-sounding names and when they reached the ocean they turned west and drove up along the coast.

Lahaina, an old whaling port in missionary days, was like a New England coastal town except for palm trees leaning tattered royal heads. They lunched on the veranda of the Pioneer Inn, an elderly white frame structure where Rita said Queen Liliuoka-lani had once stayed.

Sara had seen nothing like this on Oahu: yachts in the harbor and many bronzed men with the seas of the world in their eyes; young Establishment families, all spit and polish; artists setting up pictures under a banyan tree that took up a whole block; hip-pies with long hair and friendly faces. "We get 'em all on Maui— the Hare Krishna, the Jesus freaks," Rita told her. "The vibra-tions—the 'vibes'—are said to be better here. *Maui no ka oe*— Maui is the best, though some of the local people wish the word hadn't got around."

Sara would have liked to wander here but Rita kept looking at her watch. They drove up along the coast past strings of luxury hotels and golf courses, then turned in between gateposts whose unobtrusive brass insets announced the Aloha Nui Hotel. Swing-ing around curves of green plush where sprinklers flung rain-bows, Rita parked in front of an entrance of dark lava stone with a towering bronze statue of the god Maui throwing a lariat at the sun.

Sara had received a brochure about the hotel, but the words and pictures had not done it justice. Their schedule called for them to spend several days here and Rita, on her home island, would surely not stay with Sara all the time; in this safe place there would be no reason for her to try to enforce silly rules. Sara started to get out.

"No, don't get out yet, sweetie. This hotel rambles down all over the hillside. You might as well stay in the car, and then we can just drive around to wherever they've put us. I'll go in and find out what's what."

"Ask if I have any mail—" Sara called.

It was interesting to watch the people as she waited. Some of them were young. Some of them smiled at her with the instant friendliness that seemed to affect everyone who came here. Ten minutes passed, fifteen, before Rita came back to the car.

"No mail."

"Oh, well, I didn't expect any quite so soon."

"Furthermore, would you believe, no rooms! They had the nerve to tell me they were full up."

"But—how can that be? I thought we had reservations."

"Right." She was pulling away. "Those reservations were made a long time ago. I never dreamed it was necessary to check. There was a foul-up somehow. I don't doubt that somebody just came along and greased the old palm and that was that."

Sara turned back for a look at the beautiful Aloha Nui. "We saw a lot of other nice hotels. We can surely get rooms in one of them."

"That's what I thought. I had the reservations clerk call—that's what took me so long. Same damn story at every other decent place on this island. I couldn't believe it. But this happens to be the peak of the biggest season they've ever had."

"What are we going to do?"

"Well, that's the part I was coming to. The good part. Mr. Nielsen has been kind enough to say we can stay at his place."

It seemed to be all settled. They were driving back in the direction they had come from. A little uneasily, Sara said, "My parents do have my schedule and they think I'll be staying at the Aloha Nui. If anything should happen at home . . ."

"I took care of that, sweetie. I told them to transfer calls, if any, to the Ulewehi Ranch. *Ulewehi* means growing in beauty—isn't that charming? Oh, Sara Moore, you just don't know how lucky you are!"

"I am?" It wasn't that she didn't believe it.

"Oh, absolutely. Anybody with the price can stay with the Geritol-for-lunch bunch in the fancy tourist places with every known corny touristy touch. Nobody, but *nobody,* could ever wander onto this island and get to stay on the private estate of people who are as rich as the Nielsens. They happen to have an invalid son so they never even entertain friends any more."

"Just stranded prizewinners?"

"Right. Oh, I knew you'd be a good sport about it, sweetie."

Sara gave a philosophical shrug. "Sometimes when things seem to go wrong they turn out to be more fun. This Mr. Nielsen, is he the owner of the Valley Isle Construction and Finance Company?"

"That and half a dozen other things. He's a big industrialist with interests all over the world. He's Danish and terribly sweet. His wife is from one of the old missionary families with a dash of the *alii*—the early rulers, chiefs—thrown in. Around here, that's aristocracy with a capital A."

"It will be fun to meet people like that."

"I don't want to hold out any false hopes that you'll meet them. Mr. Nielsen is so busy and Mrs. Nielsen happens to be in Honolulu right now. I don't mind telling you that you should be glad about that."

Sara gave her a questioning look.

"My family used to live on the place when I was a kid—worked for them. The very aristocratic Mrs. Nielsen combines all the narrowness of the Boston missionaries and the royalty complexes of the *alii*. In the days of the monarchy the royal personages were considered so sacred that the *kanakas,* the common people, had to prostrate themselves when they passed by—or even when the royal bath water was carried by. Upon pain of death, no less."

"And you're really sure it's all right for us to go there?"

"Oh, yes. I talked to Mr. Nielsen personally. I mean, it's nothing to him. There are servants, of course, to do what has to be done. Our quarters will be off at the back of the house, so we won't have to bother anybody. There is even a little kitchen where we can get our own breakfast. Matter of fact, there is a young man, an employee of Mr. Nielsen's, who has a room there now."

"You mean—they rent rooms?"

Rita laughed merrily. "Oh, no, no. Mr. Nielsen just lets him stay there, since it's so hard to find a place on this island."

"What's his name?"

"Rivers. Monte Rivers. A brilliant guy. If there is anything Monte Rivers can't do, I don't know what it is. He's even got an M.D. He's not practicing any more, but it does make sense to have somebody with medical knowledge living there because of their son."

"Doesn't Dr. Rivers plan to practice?"

"No. Research is his field. He has some very advanced ideas about what can be accomplished. And he has an inventive turn of mind." She tapped the big box that lay between them. "Right now he and Mr. Nielsen are working on some adaptation of this thing—I don't understand the first thing about it—for the plane. Research grants happen to be awfully hard to get right now, but if things work out, Mr. Nielsen will finance him."

The whole setup was beginning to sound very interesting. Sara would have liked to ask Rita how old this Monte Rivers was, but she supposed she would find that out soon enough.

They had left the sea and now were driving to a higher plateau on the slope of a great mountain. Sara said, "This must be the one that's called House of the Sun—I can't pronounce it—"

"Haleakala. You accent every other syllable—HAH lay AH ka LAH. The publicity people are fond of saying that you could set Manhattan Island down inside the crater. I used to wish they would. I've never been to New York, but I'll take it sight unseen over this any day."

"But this island is fabulous!"

"Oh, it's nice enough, what there is of it. Too small for my taste. I'd prefer not to live in a place where everybody knows my business."

Sara wondered if everybody knew about Rita's affair with her boss. And if Mrs. Nielsen's current absence had anything to do with it.

They had been climbing, turning, and now the road was more narrow. This was ranch country, with Black Angus cattle grazing on pastures that were marked with outcroppings of black lava. Higher up on the mountain rose groves of ragged-barked eucalyptus trees. Near the roadside, an occasional tree had masses of orange and green fruits clustered close to the main trunk. Papaya, Rita said. At all times of the year, some of the fruit was ripe enough for eating.

They rounded a curve and Rita pointed ahead and to their left. "Look. From here we can't see the house, but we can get a good view of the drive."

Some distance ahead, a double row of dark-green cypress trees curved gracefully upward and lost itself in thick trees. It was a properly impressive approach, surely, to the home of an island millionaire.

But the enchantment lent by distance was missing when they came to the entrance. It must have been splendid once, with the tall lava-stone tiki gods on either side, but now they had tilted a little as if pulled askew by the vines. A wrought-iron sign announcing that this was the Ulewehi Ranch had a letter missing. Beneath the rise of the still-splendid cypress trees, smaller trees had grown to arch and meet overhead, making a dark tunnel over part of the driveway. The paving was bumpy, broken.

Rita shifted, drove carefully around the holes in the pavement. "They've not been back long, but all this will be fixed up, of course. In just a minute we'll be able to get a good view of the house. As you'll see, the house rambles on different levels. It used to be an old sugar plantation, and that, I think, was built on an earlier foundation that went back before the days of the white man. I have never even been in all the rooms."

She drove a little further and stopped the car. It looked at first glance, not so much like a house as a small village sprawling on several levels, enclosed under one roof and wrapped around with bushes and vines. Several mad builders might have started, stopped, changed their minds and gone their separate directions. Most of the house was built of dark stone, but Sara saw, thrusting up from a back wing on the right, what appeared to be a wooden lookout tower.

Brooding over it all was the majestic Haleakala.

"It is absolutely . . ." Sara stopped, at a loss for words. She used to dream about being a guest in a romantic house like this one.

"I knew you'd be fascinated. In its shaggy, romantic old way it has an authenticity that the slick, new places miss completely."

"But there is so much of it—"

"In the old days when it was a working ranch, I expect a couple of dozen people lived on the place. There were offices, stables, quarters for all the help. Then during the depression when money was tight they rented rooms and provided packhorses for trips up into the crater. They put in bathrooms all over the place—nothing fancy, as you'll see—but the two sisters who inherited the ranch spent about all the money they had. It failed."

"I don't see how it could."

"Well, in one way, it didn't. Mr. Nielsen came as one of the guests with a party of Danish industrialists. He married one of the sisters. She was very beautiful—still is, I suppose, if you like the haughty type."

Sara thought that maybe Mr. Nielsen had his reasons for preferring Rita after all.

Rita was pointing. "On that slope up in back, although you can't see it from here, is the remains of a *heiau,* or temple. There's not anything left of it now except some of the foundation stones. When we were kids we used to play on the slopes of the mountain, but I always avoided that place. I knew that some of our ancestors—we don't claim that they were anything but ordinary *kanakas*—may have been sacrificed there. That's how they dedicated the temples. People say that Mrs. Nielsen still believes in the old gods—I wouldn't put it past her."

Rita put the car in gear and they approached the house. You could look at most houses, Sara thought, and tell what the various rooms were. But looking up at this conglomerate, there was no way of knowing what the thick growth covered. Poinsettias grown rank leaned raggedly against the walls. Trees in wild bloom fought each other for space, crowding against each other. It was as if the house had died and the vegetation was making haste to cover and hide it, to take it back to itself so that soon it would be able to pretend no house was there as it sucked, taking nourishment from the secret parts of it.

Rita said, "In the tropics it doesn't take long for plantings to get out of hand. They've been away for a couple of years, with only a caretaker living here, mostly as a watchman. I'm sure you can imagine what everything will look like when they get it restored."

Sara was not sure she could. Rita had said that the average tourist could never hope to spend the night here, and now Sara was thinking that the average tourist probably wouldn't want to. But she was intrigued by the place, and she intended to look for that *heiau*. If she had to speak to her mother's book club, as she supposed she must, she would have a real story to tell, one that would be different from most of the dull travel talks they had to listen to.

The main driveway circled a dank pool, small and choked with waterlilies, in front of the house, but Rita was swinging off up to the right. They parked next to the house under an old tree that struggled up between cracks of bare lava. It was cool here; Sara had not known any place in Hawaii would be this cool. They took their bags in through a louvered door of faded blue into a hall where a hodgepodge of furniture, old matting, a stained mattress, had been piled against the walls.

Rita murmured about remodeling and turned right to lead the way up a long, dark hall that felt gritty underfoot, as if it needed sweeping. Shuttered windows along one side had been fastened shut, closing in a smell of dampness. A lizard streaked ahead of them and went up the wall to lose itself among the vines that had fingered their way in around the shutters.

Up three steps. Rita opened a door into a small, makeshift kitchen partitioned off from a large room that had a stone fireplace. With dismay Sara stared about her. Once the room might have been cheerful, but the bright colors of the chintz on the sofa and chairs had dimmed. A coffee cup with soggy cigarette

butts sat on a low table. Mold, gray and furry, climbed one of
the plastered walls.

"This is the living room, of course," said Rita brightly, pausing.
"Beyond, off that little hall, are a couple of bedrooms. Monte has
the one on the left. He's not here much and he's very quiet, so
that's no problem. You're upstairs—follow me!"

Sara followed her up the narrow, rickety stairs. Already her
hand touching the banister was dusty. She was beginning to wonder if she should be bothering to carry her heavy suitcase up the
stairs. Atmosphere was all very well, but she was not sure her
spirit of adventure was going to be strong enough to make her
want to spend a night in this place. Of course, she had only to
say so.

But upstairs Rita threw open a door onto a room that was
sweetly clean, with immaculate white curtains that fell to the floor.
A gem of an old brass bed shone as if from recent polishing. The
white rug on the floor looked brand-new, but some of the furniture was antique and looked as if it might have come from Boston around the Horn.

"See the view from these windows," said Rita. "There's nothing
to compare with it on the whole island."

Windows were on three sides of the room. The old tree ob-
structed the view from one of them, but from another Sara could
see the cloud-shrouded mountain, and from the third she was
able to look beyond pastures to the bright magnificence of the
Pacific far below. A small island to the southwest shone like gold
in the afternoon sun.

Sara looked around at Rita. "I noticed this place when we came
up the drive. I thought it was some kind of lookout tower—"

"That's what it was. It was open on four sides then, I suppose.
The ranch manager could look down and see if any of the cane

fields—they burn them, you know, at harvest time—had gotten out of hand. Do you like it?"

"I love it. But I don't mind telling you now that there for a minute or two I had my doubts."

Rita was looking pleased. "I'm sure you must have." She opened the doors of a large wardrobe. "There's no closet in this room, but you can hang your clothes in here. There's no real bathroom either"—she was opening another door—"and it's pretty rough, as you can see, just a toilet and sink, but you can take a shower downstairs after you get unpacked. Tonight I thought we'd go to the Sheraton-Maui. I'm going to dress up a bit. Why don't you wear that pretty dress you bought in Honolulu—since you haven't had a chance to wear it yet?"

"Good idea." Sara was not quite ready to tell Rita about the night on the town with Joe Egan, but she hadn't a doubt that she would when she got to know her a little better.

Rita started to leave the room and then turned back. "Oh, I might mention just one other thing. I told you that the Nielsens have a son who's not well. He's twenty-one. If you should happen to see him, avoid the poor thing."

"Avoid ... ?"

"Well, he has mental problems too. *Pupule,* as we say. Talks all kinds of wild nonsense. I don't mean that he's dangerous exactly, but he's weird-looking and can be a nuisance. I don't expect that you'll see him. He's with his mother. I doubt that they'll come back while we're here."

Sara glanced at Rita and turned to put a dress on a hanger. The situation was more complicated and also more interesting than it had first appeared to be. "So except for servants, the four of us are here alone—Mr. Nielsen, Monte Rivers, who invents things—"

"He's sort of helping Mr. Nielsen run the business too. For instance, Monte hired me in Honolulu. Mr. Nielsen thinks very highly of his talents." She gave Sara one of her dazzling smiles. "You just take your time and get all gorgeous, sweetie." She made kissing noises in the air.

Sara finished unpacking. It was very quiet in the room except for the *scratch-scratch* of the old tree against the screen. She went to the window and stared at the tree curiously.

It was different from any she had ever seen, gray and almost dead, rather like a misshapen old beggar man with knobbed, arthritic bones. A few big leaves flapped in the breeze like ragged garments. She turned away, not liking to look at the tree.

A thought moved into the stillness of the bright, pretty room. This room had not been readied in the last hour. It had been ready for quite a while. Waiting for her.

That was when she knew her first twinge of fear.

CHAPTER ELEVEN

Sara's uneasiness vanished as quickly as it had come. How silly to let herself think that there was anything at all odd about finding the room ready. There were servants, Rita had said. A couple of them could easily have whisked in here and cleaned the room since Rita's call. Or perhaps it had been made ready earlier for a different guest. It wasn't anything to think about twice. And she certainly wasn't going to let herself be bothered by a funny old tree just because it wasn't like anything she had ever seen back home in Illinois.

When Rita called up to say she could come down and have the first shower, she caught up towels and a robe and went right down. The bathroom was dark, but it too seemed to have been cleaned recently. She noticed shaving things on the shelf. Monte Rivers. That was an interesting name. Quiet, Rita had said; she liked quiet men. This whole thing might turn out to be fun.

She showered quickly, spoke to Rita, whom she could hear in one of the rooms beyond the bath, saying the shower was free, then hurried upstairs to put on the gold-and-blue dress she had worn with apparent success in Honolulu. Joe Egan had been fun, casual, no future, but he had given her a bit of an ego-boost. She wished she could find a flower to put in her hair.

Holding up her long dress, Sara ran downstairs. She called to Rita that she was going outside, but the shower was running and she knew Rita couldn't hear her. She went through the rooms of the little apartment, down the dark hallway with the shuttered windows. Peering through a crack between the shutters, she saw what appeared to be a garden. She found a door, opened the latch and stepped through.

It was a garden, or it had been one, enclosed on one side by a high wall, and on the others by a porch, or lanai, with rooms that opened into the main part of the house. Over her head an arching trellis sagged, broken under the weight of a monstrous vine which in its coddled infancy might have been supported by the trellis and encouraged to climb. Like a spoiled child, the vine had grown to become overweight and strong, crushing its support, leaping to catch with muscular arms the two trees which stood on either side. They leaned together now in a strange dead embrace while the murdering vine still reached for more of the garden.

Sara stepped out from under the vine, disentangling a tendril which clutched at her hair. Almost no light penetrated the garden. She looked up; the rank growth of still more vines and flowering trees almost hid the blue of the sky. The air did not move. It was heavy enough to taste, with the rotted sweetness of too many flowers that had bloomed and died, as in a funeral chapel where there have been too many funerals. And as in such a place, sadness was thick.

She was, she realized, vaguely uneasy.

Foolish. She wanted only one flower for her hair and they bloomed here in almost an obscenity of profusion. But they were all so big. They leaned toward her with wide mouths flaring, breathing on her with their heavy, almost anesthetizing perfume. Even the colors were overpowering, ranging from brilliant scarlet, as if full of young blood, to a purple that reminded her of the ribbons on a funeral wreath.

With care she stepped along what had once been a path, feeling that she should not make any sound. In the center, almost hidden, she noticed a greening-bronze fountain. It was dead, with no water flowing. A smiling stone child raised sightless eyes and outstretched arms to the place where the water should have come from, but more vines, not water, reached for the hands.

Sara averted her eyes from the child's body, scabbed and leprous with lichen, and saw a rose bush near the child's feet. The blooms were small, wax-pale, as if the bush were losing the fight for sun and air.

She picked one rose, inhaled the gentle scent. It looked like a small, frail sister of the Peace roses Dr. Durham had brought her in the hospital. The scent was similar too, taking her back for a moment to the dull safety of those days.

Someone was watching her. She had not been aware of any sound, but she looked around quickly. A man, Viking-tall, with heavy gunmetal hair, had come out of one of the doors that opened to the lanai from the main house.

Mr. Nielsen, of course. Sara started to go toward him, ready with a smile and appropriate words of thanks. "Mr. Nielsen, I—" She stopped, the smile dying on her lips.

He looked at her with the saddest eyes she had ever seen, turned abruptly and went into the house.

Rita acted a little annoyed when Sara told her about it. "Well,

I must say I'd a little rather you hadn't gone barging like that into their private quarters."

"Just the garden—all I wanted was one flower for my hair." She felt like taking it out now and throwing it away. "Mr. Nielsen could surely spare one little flower from all that tangled mess. And he could have been courteous."

"Well, he's got a lot of problems right now. Or maybe the phone started ringing in the house or something. With his wife away, I expect he'd hurry to answer it. He's really a very sweet man, so don't worry about it." Rita was all ready in a gown of flaming coral that displayed her splendid cleavage. "Never mind. I'll explain later about your being in the garden."

Later—in his arms? The one glimpse Sara had had of that tall somber-faced man now made that very hard to believe. She wondered if Monte Rivers was the one.

"Let's go. I've made reservations for seven."

They drove back down to civilization.

Sara felt dimmed by Rita as they walked past the guests at the Sheraton-Maui. Several men spoke to her, some with an almost leering familiarity.

Rita answered modestly if at all, with a ladylike averting of her glance. "Some of the men on this island are impossible," she murmured as she steered Sara past them to a table. When a cheerful chap with interested glances at Sara leaned to say, "Hi, Rita, long time no see—" she said, "I've been away," and turned her back. "Do try a Sundowner, sweetie. And while we're waiting I want to tell you the history of the hill on which this hotel was built."

Interested though she was in history, Sara looked at the retreating figure a little wistfully. The duenna again, she thought, and gave her attention to Rita's story.

"Nobody knows what happened to the temple that was supposed to have been on this spot, but by the time of the last king of Maui, the people had become convinced that the whole area was haunted."

Sara rested her chin on folded hands. "Good. It will take a ghost story to divert me."

"Divert—?"

Sara gestured with her head in the direction the young man had gone. "I wouldn't object, you know, to meeting some nice, nifty guy while I'm on Maui. Men at home are scarce as hen's teeth."

"Nice ones are just as scarce here, sweetie. And that fellow isn't anybody you'd care about knowing. Very dull. Now, do you want to hear about this place or not?"

"I'm listening. Go on." She started sipping the heady concoction that had been set before her.

"Well, the people also thought that the cave below called Moe-moe—which means Lie down to sleep—was inhabited by evil ghosts who would never let anybody escape. When the king saw that his people's terror made them neglect their taro patches here and kept them from swimming along this beach, he told them that he would take the 'leap of death' from that rock over there and swim past the haunted cave to prove they had nothing to fear. So with all the people wailing, he dived from the rock." She spread her hands and smiled. "He returned safely, and as all good Island stories end, there was much joy and feasting. Now, watch over there and you'll see the whole thing reenacted."

Offshore the islands of Molokai and Lanai were mauve under the fierce sunlit glory of orange and black clouds. At the mournful, musical sound of the conch shell, a beachboy ran to set the torches aflame along the top of the cliff. When he had lighted the last torch, he cast his fire aside and for a moment was silhouetted blackly against the dimming sky as he dived from the rock into the sea.

Some of the guests had movie cameras, and Sara wished she had one too. It wasn't going to be easy to describe the drama with mere words. The food that followed wasn't going to be easy to describe either—she was sure her parents had never eaten mahi-mahi macadamia or passion fruit pie. Some of the symbolism of the native dances in the floor show was lost on her, but she was mesmerized by the whirling and swirling of the red and yellow feathered gourds.

On the way back to the Ulewehi Ranch, Sara said dreamily, "I have to pinch myself. I can't believe this is me. This time last week I was at home, living in a house where I know every piece of furniture, every rug, window, and door so well I could find my way blindfolded. I know the whole town almost that well. I know all the people and why they do what they do and what they're going to do. Like, across the street there is this old man who sweeps his porch at five o'clock every morning and turns his lights off at nine o'clock at night."

"Deliver me."

"Me too. Here I have the feeling . . . well, that I've been put down in the middle of a movie and I can't figure out the plot because I don't know what's gone before."

"Oh, I don't think there was anything too difficult about any of that tonight. The torch ceremony was just a reenactment—I explained that—and the floor show was only—"

"No, no, I don't mean that. Other things. Take Mr. Nielsen— why are his eyes so sad?"

Rita took her eyes off the road for a moment to glance at Sara, laughing a little. "You know what I think? I think there's such a thing as having too much imagination. I told you Mr. Nielsen has a few problems, but I don't let myself wonder about what they are because I figure they aren't any of my business. And they're not any of your business either, sweetie, so why don't you just relax?"

"Oh, I am relaxed, but I'm just so curious. That house fascinates me. There's something just a little scary—"

"Nonsense."

"Yes, there is. It's kind of fun in a way—I've always liked mysteries—but I sense something there that I don't quite . . . for instance, when I went into the garden—"

"That's easy. Stay out of the garden." They had reached the looming tiki gods of the entrance, and as Rita turned in and started under the dark tunnel of trees she said, "I realize this place may look a little bit spooky, but I promise you there are no ghosts. The Nielsens may not be quite like anybody you know back in Woodsriver, and I'm sure the house is different, but you just stay where you belong and everything will be fine. Where would you like to go tomorrow?"

"I don't know. My guidebook says Hana is a must."

"Oh, yes. They call it Heavenly Hana. We ought to allow the whole day for that. It's pretty slow driving, but the scenery is magnificent, with lots of places to stop. On that part of the island there are probably more full-blooded Hawaiians than anywhere else. The Hotel Hana Ranch is considered one of the luxury resorts of the world—very different from anything you've seen. Below that is a lovely place called the Seven Sacred Pools. I think I can promise you a day that will take your mind off whatever is bothering you about this place."

"Oh, I didn't mean that I don't like staying here."

"Well, it's a roof over our heads. We really are extremely lucky, you know." She parked the Mercedes under the old gray tree and they went inside.

Sara was looking forward to meeting Monte Rivers. Rita might not be very helpful about introducing her to any of the men on the island, but she could hardly keep her from meeting the man who was staying in the same part of the house with them.

He was not there, and any idea Sara might have had about hanging around to meet him was dispelled by Rita's quick assurance that she must be very tired. "Here, sweetie, you said you liked mysteries—take this little paperback up to bed with you and read yourself to sleep."

Sara took the book and went up. It was obvious that Rita was eager to get rid of her. She cleared a space on her dressing table and wrote a letter to her parents, telling them about the evening at the Sheraton-Maui and about this house. She realized when she read the page of description she had written about the walled garden that she had made it sound sinister, so she tore it up and wrote, "It's a romantic place with a fountain in the center and enormous flowers. Some of them must be six inches across." And then, "I have seen the owner, Mr. Nielsen, but I have not met him yet..."

She couldn't get much interested in Rita's book. The palace in Rome with its marble pilasters had less reality for her than the scabbed stone boy in this garden here. And the heroine was too much like what she had always thought herself to be, too meek and eager to please. Sara liked to read for escape, not identification.

She turned out the light and tried to go to sleep. But the old tree scratched against the screen, and the events of the day went round and round in her mind. As in the hospital, where she had whiled away so many boring hours watching soap operas, she caught herself investing simple situations with drama that wasn't there at all: beautiful, enigmatic Rita, was she having an affair with the brilliant young scientist Monte Rivers? Or with the rich Mr. Nielsen, whose wife had left, heartbroken . . . ?

Enough of that. Sara gave a thump to her pillow. Mrs. Nielsen's absence very likely had something to do with refurbishing the house. And anyhow, as Rita had told her plainly enough, it was none of her business. So that was that. The bed was comfortable and she was really very tired.

Pre-sleep images began to float behind her closed lids. She saw a tangle of geometric lines which became the interlacing vines over the garden. They began to writhe, to lunge, trying to snare the sun with their green lariats. Under the darkening sky she saw the stone child turn, arms out, and move toward her smiling as the tears fell from his sightless eyes.

A car stopped down below Sara's window and she woke. Almost at once she heard Rita's voice as if she had been watching for the car and hurried outside.

"Oh, God, Monte, where have you been? I thought you'd never come. Is everything all set?"

"Christ. All set?—the valve is busted."

"Oh, no!"

"You must have dropped the goddamned thing, Rita. I told you to be careful with it."

"I didn't drop it, Monte, I swear! I held it on my lap the whole way. You can fix it, can't you?"

"I don't know. I'll get to work on it first thing tomorrow. If I can't fix it, I'll have to go to Honolulu on Monday and get them to put on another valve with that special fitting."

He might be a genius, as Rita had implied, but he didn't sound very attractive, and the talk about valves had no interest to Sara.

She turned over in bed and wished that old tree out there would quit making that noise so she could get back to sleep.

From downstairs now she heard the breaking-glass sound of ice cubes being released from their tray. There was the murmuring of voices, their cadences changed as they moved from the kitchen.

So that was settled. She was sure now that it had been Monte Rivers to whom Rita talked on the phone that night in Honolulu. Since seeing the sad-eyed Mr. Nielsen it had been hard to visualize him in the role of Rita's lover. Perhaps Monte Rivers too had money for diamond watches. Sara yawned. Certainly it had nothing to do with her.

It sounded as if another car was coming up the long drive. But that had nothing to do with her either.

CHAPTER TWELVE

It would be a help, Sara thought, if she knew more about what she was looking for. Stones, Rita had said, the foundation of the ancient *heiau*. But the ground up here was broken by lava outcroppings and many scattered stones, none of which seemed to have any order. Whether she found it or not, she was glad the search for it had brought her out here. She felt that private, virtuous joy that comes to early risers. At the moment, she owned the morning: nobody seemed to be stirring yet down at the house; no vehicles moved on the road above or the one below; no ships were visible far below on the ocean.

The chattering of the little wild mynah birds had wakened her before the first rays of the sun came over Haleakala. With haste, she had dressed in shirt and shorts and put on sneakers. As she left the house quietly, she noted that a little green Saab which she supposed belonged to Monte Rivers was parked beside the white Mercedes. She had made her way through the daffodil light past a scattering of unused barns and stables and started up the slope. It seemed important not to waste one hour of this day, for if a room should become available at one of the hotels this would be her last day at Ulewehi Ranch.

The cool air had a fresh, clean smell here under the uncluttered sky. A mongoose, long-tailed, dirty tan, ran ahead of her, its little weasel-like body close to the ground. A small red bird perched on a tree that flowered with identical red. Nothing was familiar, not even herself. She felt as if her blood had quickened to the special vibrations of the island of Maui.

The red bird flashed ahead of her, revealing black wings and gray underneath. It disappeared into a luxuriant thicket, and as she neared it she saw one reason for all the vegetation. A huge wooden reservoir, barrel-shaped, leaked a little, spilled over the top a little. No doubt it was fed from springs further up the mountain.

From here Sara could look back down at the sprawling house. Most of the rooms, as she had thought, clustered around the walled garden. At the side of the house, opposite where she had slept, she saw the rectangular shape of a large swimming pool. It was empty now, although this reservoir could have filled it easily.

She tried to imagine the place with guests swimming in that pool, strolling from room to room, laughing and talking as they wandered through that garden, but it was a little difficult. She wondered why it was that people with the Nielsens' wealth had wanted to move in before the remodeling had been done. She would probably never learn the answers, but it was interesting to have had even a brief glimpse into the sort of world she had never known.

A pipeline led upward from the reservoir and Sara followed it into a little gully where tree ferns grew high overhead. Some flower—she could not be sure which one of several—bloomed with a spicy perfume. But here where the flowers could bloom and die and be composted naturally in the thick, springy humus underfoot, there was no smell of death.

A bird that looked like a pheasant rose with a whirr of wings that startled her. Somewhere ahead she could hear the soft splashing of water. She followed the pipe until she came to the place where the water spilled in a thin sheet of crystal over dark rocks into a shadowed pool. More ferns uncoiled their graceful fronds, growing high like green tatted lace. Fuchsias and flowers resembling the bleeding hearts at home leaned over the dark mirror of the pool. She wondered if they grew wild, or if they had been planted here by someone who loved the place.

She knelt at the edge of the pool, drank and washed her face; in time past, Hawaiian girls must have done the same.

A face looked at her from behind the curtain of water. A small image stood there in a little grotto, its expression gentler than most, the eyes as luminous as if they had been made of pearl shell. Blossoms were heaped at the feet of the little god, so fresh that they might have been placed there only minutes before.

Who had placed the flowers there and with what prayers? What did one ask of a small gentle god who almost smiled from his niche behind the water?

In the green silence around her, there was the merest sibilance of leaves, a vibrating of curiosity, a friendly waiting for answers: *Who is this girl?*

She had yet to know. But as she walked back into the open brightness of the morning she knew who she was not. She was not a girl who would ever again believe it was living to thump out little pieces on the piano for other people's children, to rock on the porch with her parents, to crawl through pine needles looking for some old lady's dentures, content with the clapping of dry old hands. All that was good. It would never again be good enough.

The breeze lifted her hair and dried her face and hands as she started back down the slope by a different route. The red bird had reappeared. It paused on a pile of stones. No, not a pile. They had been cut and fitted together at some time, making a long rectangle that was squared at the base and rose in some places to a height of two or three feet, slanting inward. Some of them were broken and scattered now, but there was a sort of platform. It could have been the foundation for almost any sort of building, but she felt that it must be the old *heiau*. She climbed over the stones, trying to imagine the human sacrifices that might have taken place here, with Maui chiefs in feathered cloaks and priests who believed in a god who must be appeased by blood.

A flash of light caught her eye. From an upstairs window of the main part of the house below, someone was looking at her through binoculars.

She jumped down from the stone blocks and started back down the slope. She had not been able to see the watcher, and the binoculars had disappeared now from the window. Was it Mr. Nielsen, who had turned so abruptly last night as if he didn't want her here? She hoped it hadn't been another invasion of privacy for her to climb around on the foundations of the old temple.

It might be just as well if she and Rita did move on from here today.

Coming around the outbuildings, she almost collided with someone. He was tall, very tall, and almost skeleton-thin. He was young. Binoculars dangled from a strap around his neck. Startled, she stepped back.

He fingered the binoculars, smiling down at her. Under bright chestnut hair, his large eyes were the color of tarnished silver. "Did I frighten you?"

"Yes, a little." She was breathless. "I didn't expect to see anybody out here at this hour."

"I'm Chris Nielsen. My mother and I got back late last night from Honolulu. We were supposed to stay several days longer, but she got one of her sudden hunches. I'm glad. I hate to be away from this place." His grin showed perfect white teeth that looked too large for his thin, tanned face. "Especially when girls like you are wandering around."

A little nervously she told him her name. "I won a contest sponsored by your father's company—you probably know about that—"

"No, he never talks business. It bores me."

"Well, there was a mix-up about reservations and your father said we could stay here last night. I was up there just now on that foundation—"

"The *heiau*. It's a fascinating place. Sometimes at night I have seen light moving up there. I have heard drums. Not long ago I was sure I heard the sound of wailing for the dead. They make a sound like this—" He put back his head. "Auweau-we-e-e."

The hair on Sara's scalp lifted just a little. She gave him an uncertain smile and started to walk on. Rita had told her.

"Don't go, Sara Moore. Help me try to find the crested honeycreeper. Just a minute ago I thought I saw one up there. They're very rare, you know."

"The—what?"

"Crested honeycreeper. They're black with orange streaks. They have a crest at the base of their upper bill. They're of the family of *Drepanididae*."

"Hawaiian words—" she began.

"Oh, that's Latin. The Hawaiian name is *nukupuu*. Until 1967 this bird was thought to be extinct."

"Really?" She said it politely. "I saw a red bird with black wings."

"That's the *apapane*. They like the lehua trees, the ones with the red flowers."

"Oh? Well, I'm afraid I'm not much of a bird watcher." She felt a little sorry for him, but she was not about to walk back up the slope with this weird boy.

He swung into step beside her. "Not everyone is interested in birds. What about stars, are you interested in stars? The Hawaiians studied astronomy hundreds of years ago. I've got a little observatory shack rigged up over there. Every night when I'm here, that's where I go. You can just barely see it from here—it's out there beyond the ridge of lava—"

Sara stood on tiptoe to look where he was pointing. "Yes, I can see a sort of dome. I think I remember seeing that from my window up there."

"One of the astronomers from up at Science City helped me rig it up when we were here two years ago. It isn't a real observatory, of course, but when we came back last month I brought back a pretty good telescope that my parents gave me for my twenty-first birthday. It's a reflector type with a short focal length. A Questar —what they call a comet seeker. Did you know that if you discover a comet you can have it named for you?"

"No, I didn't happen to know that, Chris." She gave him a smile. He was definitely odd, and certainly not like any twenty-one-year-old she had ever known, but she wasn't afraid of him. His deep tan didn't disguise the blue tinge of his lips, and she saw that his nails were blue-tinged too. He breathed with an apparent effort, as if he might have asthma.

"I'd like to talk to you later if you have the time. I don't get much of a chance to talk to girls my own age—I seem to put them off somehow—but I bet you and I could find something to talk about."

"I bet we could, Chris, even though I'm twenty-five."

"I like older women." There was something appealing about his grin.

"I'll probably see you around later. I really have to go in now—I've not had any breakfast yet."

The green Saab was gone. In the little kitchen a pot of coffee, still warm, sat on the hot plate. Sara saw a cup that had held coffee—again, with soggy cigarette butts—and a bowl that looked as if it had been used for cereal. So once more—not that she was interested now—she had missed catching a glimpse of Monte Rivers. Rita, she supposed, was still sleeping.

Sara was starved. While the coffee heated she ate some fresh pineapple that she found in the refrigerator. There was not enough milk left for cereal, so she made a couple of slices of toast and found some butter and jam. Not wanting to eat down here where it was so dreary, she took a tray up to her room and put it on the window sill, where she could look at the view.

A voice floated up. "Morning, sweetie. I heard you stirring around. Find some breakfast?"

"Sure. I'm fine. Just drinking my coffee up here and admiring the view."

"Good girl. Well, I think I'll take a cup of coffee and go back to bed. It's only eight o'clock. But pretty soon we'll get ready and go out."

Sara was about to go downstairs to see if there was any coffee left when she heard the kitchen door open. Quick steps crossed the living room and went toward the bedrooms beyond. A voice spoke with authority, "So it's you here, Rita Gomez. Get dressed and get out. I see you have your suitcase here. Pack it and leave at once."

"Oh, Mrs. Nielsen, you don't understand—"

"That's quite right. I certainly do not understand what you are doing in my house. I have known something was going on. This is not a hotel—certainly not that kind of hotel. Hurry and get out of that bed. Kimo will drive you."

Not a hotel. Sara had tiptoed softly to the door to listen. She would go too, of course.

Rita was saying something about having left a book upstairs. She came up and put a finger to her lips. "Sh-h. Don't let her know you're here."

Sara put the book into Rita's hands. "But—"

Rita shushed her, whispered that she would be in touch, and went downstairs. For a moment after the kitchen door had closed on them both, Sara just sat there, stunned.

CHAPTER THIRTEEN

She would have to leave. She wasn't even going to wait for Rita to "get in touch." Mr. Nielsen's attitude last night should have clued her in. Chris, that poor friendly boy, did not matter.

Sara started throwing things into her bag any old way, and then she stopped. *Leave?* She was miles from anywhere. She wouldn't want to try to carry her heavy suitcase all the way down that long lane even if she knew there was bus service at the entrance gates. What did Rita expect her to do—just hide here? She didn't want to get Rita into any more trouble, but this was a terrible spot to be in and she meant to get out of it.

She had not happened to notice a telephone downstairs, but she knew there must be one. If she could call for a taxi now and then finish packing while she waited for it to come...

She ran downstairs. There was no phone in the living room and none in the kitchen. She went into the hall beyond the living room and looked through the open door of the bedroom on the right. No phone. The room was in perfect order. Rita could have hardly tidied it so neatly in so little time. Mrs. Nielsen must have found her in the bed in the other room where Monte Rivers—he of the soggy cigarette butts—would no doubt have left his clothes strewn around.

Sara groaned. She had heard a touch of the Boston missionary— yes, and the *alii* too—in those crisp commands to get out of the house.

But the door to that room was closed and also locked. She knew the phone must be in there! Why was it locked? She rattled the knob with exasperation. She had to get to a telephone. She thought, If I could just find Chris . . .

She opened the kitchen door carefully and peered down the long, shuttered hall; it was empty. Without a sound she went to the end of it, opened the louvered door and looked out. The Mercedes was gone and there was no sign of Chris.

The garden door was here and also another. It must lead to the rest of the house, perhaps the kitchen, where there would surely be a telephone. It was almost too much to hope that nobody would see her.

But the hall that continued beyond the door had a look of disuse also. She looked into one room that seemed as if it had once been an office. Another was jammed with old furniture, and still another held saddles and other riding equipment that had the appearance of having been stored for all the years since the place was a working ranch.

Steps led down, accommodating the house to the slope, and beyond them she saw another door. She paused, her hand on the knob. What a dilemma, opening doors like this and not knowing at what moment she might be confronted by the angry mistress of the house. She turned the knob.

Here the hall turned to the right; it was wider, with evidence of being well cared for. A flight went up, looking like back stairs. She saw also a small elevator. Naturally they would have one if Chris was asthmatic.

Small bedrooms opening off this hall told her this was the servants' wing. With luck, they would be busy elsewhere at this time of day. Sara moved quickly, for she spied a phone on the wall at the end of this hall beside still another door.

Two directories were tucked into a niche under the phone, a large one for Honolulu and a small one that said MAUI, MOLOKAI and LANAI. Her fingers fumbled through the yellow pages. She dialed the number of the largest ad, realizing that when the taxi came she wouldn't have the slightest idea where to go, nor how to get in touch with Rita Gomez. But getting out of here right now was the main thing. Then she'd be able to collect her scattered wits.

"Aloha! Kaanapali Taxi—"

"Aloha. I wonder if I can get a taxi to pick me up at—"

The door beside her opened. A tall woman stood there. She had silvery blond hair drawn high. "I'm Mrs. Nielsen. Please tell me what is going on in my house."

Sara put back the phone. "I—was calling for a taxi to come and pick me up. I—am Sara Moore, Mrs. Nielsen. There were no rooms available at the hotels yesterday, and your husband very kindly said I could stay here. I won—"

"Yes, yes. I was just talking to my son upstairs and he told me all that. He said he had seen you earlier. I do not understand any of this at all. I know I must sound extremely lacking in courtesy. It is not that I don't believe what you say is true, but my husband has gone out, and until he comes back I hardly know what I should do." She was breathing hard as if agitated.

Sara faltered, "I understand how you must feel. Coming back and finding strangers—"

The chin lifted. "Rita Gomez is not a stranger. I do not know if you heard that unpleasant scene back there or not. Her family used to live on the place—fine people, with that one exception. She most certainly is not welcome here."

She touched Sara's arm. "I have embarrassed you, I know. Please forgive me. I know nothing about my husband's business affairs, but I do know I don't have to have that woman under my roof. But let's not stand here. Come and sit down with me where we can be more comfortable."

Sara followed her past a kitchen and pantries. Mrs. Nielsen opened still another door and they were in a wide paneled hall that had something of the look of the Bishop Museum. French doors at intervals on the right opened onto the walled garden. On their left was a dining room, and beyond that a very large room which was in almost total darkness, with dust sheets on sofas and chairs.

The next room was small, more intimate. The vines had been cleared from the windows, showing a cheerful mixture of rattan furniture and carved teak. Delicate watercolors decorated the walls and a Chinese vase held peacock feathers.

While Mrs. Nielsen spoke to a maid in the hall, Sara crossed to the windows to look out on a scene that was different from the one she saw from her room. Beyond the broad front lanai, past the sloping pastures, the West Maui mountains rose with a view of the ocean on either side.

"Mei-ling will bring us some coffee in a moment. Please sit down."

"I really must not take very much time."

"A few minutes will surely make no difference. I believe my son told me that you are staying in what we call the lookout room. I had not known it was habitable."

"Why, yes, it's very clean, a delightful room." Here in the bright light, Mrs. Nielsen had the look of someone who never went out in the sun, although there was an olive hue to her skin that contrasted strikingly with her pale hair. The eyes on Sara were like Chris's, though with a little more tarnish to the silver.

"I cannot imagine how . . . well, never mind, I am sure my husband will be able to explain everything when he comes home tonight. Meanwhile, let me say that I am glad you like the room. My sister and I took over those quarters for a while after our parents died. It was a happy room. I was a very romantic young girl in those days. I used to look out the window down to the ocean and dream that my prince would come on one of those great liners we used to see. He did, of course, but that was a long time ago." She smiled, looking neither royal nor Bostonian.

An elderly maid came with a tray.

"Thank you, Mei-ling." Mrs. Nielsen started pouring coffee into translucent china cups.

"Now, tell me a little about yourself, Sara Moore. That's a pretty name. It has the sound of 'forevermore,' and that is said to be one of the most melodious words in the English language."

How kind she is, thought Sara, to be trying to put me at ease.

"You are not married, I see." Mrs. Nielsen's eyes were on Sara's left hand. "I'm sure there must be a young man waiting."

"Somewhere." It was easy somehow to say that to Mrs. Nielsen.

"And that's another beautiful word, isn't it?"

"Yes, it is." Some of the good feeling of the early morning had come back.

"I was older than you, I'm sure, when I married. Where is your home?"

Sara told her. They talked for a while about Woodsriver and what life was like in a small Midwestern town. In spite of what Rita had told her about Mrs. Nielsen, Sara found herself drawn to her. She had dignity but also the unpretentious friendliness of the people back home.

Sara finished her coffee and stood up, not wanting to overstay her welcome. "Thank you for the coffee, Mrs. Nielsen. I really must go now."

"Kimo will be back soon. He will take you wherever you want to go, though you are welcome to continue staying here if you should decide you would like to. I shall talk to my husband when he comes back tonight. I have never concerned myself at all with his business, but I am sure I shall understand everything when he explains it to me. Come, let me show you a few of our things as we go through the hall."

The paneling, she said, was koa wood, cut from trees on the place more than a hundred years ago. The very long rug that went all the way to the curving staircase at the end of the hall had come from China. Mrs. Nielsen stopped before the portrait of a dark-skinned woman with wavy black hair and beautiful features. She was dressed in clothes that must have been worn by fashionable women everywhere in the early days of Queen Victoria's reign.

"She was my great-grandmother. You see, not all of them were fat."

They paused beside a large glass case where a feather cloak had been spread. "This is only a fragment, badly damaged, and about half the size of what it was originally. If it were in better condition, I should feel that I had to give it to a museum, and perhaps someday I shall. All the designs were different, as you may know. You can see how tiny the feathers are, like silken stitches. No one knows when the first one was made, nor how it came to be that generations would be willing to work so long to make just one cloak."

"Did the birds have to be killed?"

"No, they were snared and then let go after a few feathers, perhaps only two, were taken from each bird. The early Hawaiians had ideas about ecology that we would do well to remember. For instance, when they brought a plant down from the mountains they knew that the next time they returned they must take another to replace it."

"But the sandalwood—"

"Yes, that's nearly all gone. Greed came with the white man. The people here had not known it before."

"The missionaries—?"

"Oh, no. The original missionaries, almost without exception, died poor, contrary to what you may have heard. Some of their children did well, but when you consider that they had inherited the boldness of spirit it took to sail around the Horn in those small ships—" She gave a little laugh. "Oh, I am very defensive of both sides of my ancestry, Sara, although there is much I do not understand."

She passed on to another case. "That pendant there on the tapa is made of human bone, or so the experts have told me. That neck piece was made from teeth—perhaps from conquered enemies, I don't know. Next to it is a nose flute and another early instrument called a *ukeke*. In this case on the wall is a Bible that belonged to my great-great-grandfather, one of the first to come to Maui. Beside it you see a letter which he wrote back to Boston telling about what he considered to be the obscenity of the hula."

Images stood at intervals about the hall. Some were grinning;

some looked fierce; and one had a wide-open mouth as if he would scream forever at the injustices done to the Hawaiian people.

Sara said hesitantly, "This morning very early I went up the mountain slope. Up where the pipeline leads. And I found such a lovely pool and a sheet of water and behind it—oh, I know I was trespassing—I saw a small stone image."

"I'm glad you found it. I go there often. I do not know what that little fellow represents—there were so many gods—but there is a gentleness about him that I love."

"Fresh flowers were at his feet."

"Yes, I put them there just before I went to Honolulu. They stay fresh for a long time with the cool mist all around them." Her face had the sadness that Sara had seen in Mr. Nielsen's eyes last night as she said, "I pray to all the gods. I pray to Christ and His mother and all the saints. To the great Akua, but . . ."

She put a smile on her face. "Do feel free to stay here if you like, my dear."

They reached the end of the hall. Sara said, "Thank you for your kindness, Mrs. Nielsen. This place is so fascinating, so beautiful. And when you have restored it—"

"Oh, no, Sara." The sadness came back. "We will never restore Ulewehi."

CHAPTER FOURTEEN

Kimo came back.

In her room, after she had taken a shower, Sara put on a white jersey dress and got ready to go out just as if she knew where she was going.

In spite of Mrs. Nielsen's kindness, she did not know what she should do. The sensible thing right now was to have Kimo take her to the Valley Isle Construction and Finance Company and get everything straightened out with Mr. Nielsen. Rita would probably be there. At least he would know where she could be found.

Rita . . . what was so bad about Rita Gomez that Mrs. Nielsen had ordered her out of the house?

She put on white sandals. She was not crazy about her traveling companion, but she could hardly continue her fifteen days without her unless she wanted to spend her own money and take chances of getting reservations on the other islands.

Sara sat at the mirror putting a little make-up on the bright tan that seemed to be hiding her freckles. Considering her situation, she realized that the most sensible thing would be to forfeit the rest of the trip and go home. But the bleakness that came with that thought was answer enough.

She wished she knew someone she could ask for advice. Not her parents. If she called them she was sure their answer would be a fast two words: Come home. She wished she knew someone on this island, reliable, disinterested...

Of course. Relieved, she reached for her bag and looked up the addresses of the doctors that Dr. Durham had given her. Dr. David Choy was the one on Maui. His office was in Kahului.

Kimo was a pleasant young man with limited English, so they couldn't talk very much.

"Dr. Choy? The best—da kine. Rita Gomez? Shame my face, da kine."

A girl in a nurse's white pantsuit, black hair piled tall, took Sara's name in Dr. Choy's office. No appointment? She looked doubtful as she reached for a form. "If you will just fill this out, please—"

"No, no, I'm not going to be a patient. There's nothing wrong with me. I just wanted to see Dr. Choy on a personal matter. No, I don't know him, but Dr. Gilbert Durham in St. Louis gave me his name."

"Well, on Saturday many of the doctors are not in their offices, so we're jammed. But if you want to wait—"

She took a seat in the crowded waiting room. Eleven came; eleven-thirty. She drew pictures for a solemn, black-eyed boy while his mother went inside; talked to a very old man with a dark face and white hair who told her she must see the Iao Needle. "You go Wailuku. Then my house on the road, pink, all the flowers; you stop by." A man who had a playboy look told her he was staying at the Hilton and asked where she was staying, his eyes making a happy tour of her figure. "Ulewehi Ranch." He had never heard of it.

It was after twelve before the waiting room was cleared and the office nurse, apologizing for the long wait, told Sara she could come into Dr. Choy's office.

A funny-looking little doctor sat hunched around a telephone, his face turned away from her as he wrote left-handed on a pad. Without looking up, he waved her to a chair, said, "Fine . . . continue the i. v. . . . sounds good . . ." into the phone, then hung up and looked at her.

Only his black hair was funny-looking, all cowlicks. His face, now that she could see it, gave her a jolt. It had that golden look, with a fineness of chiseling that could have been Chinese, and a strength that could have been Hawaiian. She remembered hearing that some Irishmen had once swum ashore—wherever it came from, he could have made a living with his smile.

His black-brown eyes were warm as he took a deep breath of relaxation and leaned back with his hands folded behind his shaggy head. "I don't know any Dr. Gilbert Durham in St. Louis."

"I know. He looked you up in that A.M.A. thing." She launched into the necessary explanations, ending up with the fact that she was staying at the Ulewehi Ranch.

"You are?" His brows came together. "At Christian Nielsen's?"

"Yes. Is there anything wrong with the Nielsens?"

"Oh, no. They're great people. I had heard that they were back, but I didn't suppose they'd be having any guests these days. They've had some problems."

"Yes, I gathered. The son doesn't seem to be very well."

He nodded. "Well, you're extremely lucky to have been invited to stay there. I am just surprised that they would open their home to—you should excuse the dirty word—a tourist. You get an entirely different slant on any new place when you're invited into a private home. I found that out when I was invited into some of the doctors' homes in Baltimore when I was in medical school there." He started clearing his desk, clipping scattered papers together and putting them into file folders. "But how come a nice girl like you—" He frowned, looking into his drawer for paper clips.

Oh, no, thought Sara. Not that old . . .

"—was at the Sheraton last night with Rita Gomez?"

She stared at him.

"I was there last night. You were in the Discovery Room, weren't you, around nine o'clock?"

Sara nodded. "Yes, but I didn't see you."

"The place was pretty crowded, but I noticed you especially because you reminded me of a *haole* girl I almost married in Baltimore—except you're prettier. I was wondering if there wasn't some way I could get to meet you—and then I saw you were with Rita Gomez. So I said to myself, Forget it."

"What is *wrong* with Rita Gomez?"

"Rita is an extremely bright girl. Grades got her a college scholarship."

"*Please.*"

He went on clipping papers together for a minute. "If Rita were my patient and you asked me what was wrong with her medically I would not tell you—not even if all she had wrong with her was an ingrown toenail. But you have come here as a friend of a colleague and I make haste to tell you that Rita Gomez is completely without scruples and will do anything for money. Rita made a stag movie when she was fourteen." He shrugged. "She was poor and pretty and so—well, maybe. But that was just the beginning."

He folded his hands together and leaned back to look at her gravely. "She has busted up two marriages that I know of. Her own mother kicked her out of the house. She had a child—nobody knew whose—and a year ago last winter I happened to be called in when that child was brought into the hospital half dead with ribs cracked and bruises you wouldn't believe. The X-rays showed old bone breaks. I would have welcomed the chance to testify, but for some reason no charges were brought and her mother took the child. My God, Sara Moore, how come you're mixed up with Rita Gomez?"

Sara let out the breath she had been holding. She said faintly, "Wow," and gave a little shake to clear her head. "That's a lot to take in all at once. All I know is that she was the one who met me in Honolulu. She works for Mr. Nielsen—something about Public Relations. She is handling everything about my trip. I can't say I like her very much, but we've managed to get along well enough, and then this morning Mrs. Nielsen kicked her out."

"Oh, don't tell me that a man like Christian Nielsen is—no, no, of course not. But I can't understand why he would even have her working for him."

"Somebody else hired her."

"Even so, it just doesn't figure. Of course, I don't think the story of the child is generally known, and anyhow the Nielsens were away when that happened. So let's give him the benefit of the doubt."

Thinking back, Sara said slowly, "I am sure Rita cleared it with him for me to stay there, but I couldn't understand why he wasn't more friendly when he saw me. Mrs. Nielsen couldn't have been nicer this morning—to me, that is—but she didn't seem to understand things either."

"One of the things that I can't understand is about those reservations, that no-room business. I know some of those people at the Aloha Nui. Let me check it out."

He picked up the phone, hunched around it again, and talked to somebody named Jan. "What is it with you people out there—no rooms? . . . Yes, yes, I know, but there was supposed to be an advance reservation starting yesterday for a Miss Sara Moore. Could you check on that for me, Jan?"

"The reservations might have been made in Rita's name," Sara suggested while he waited.

He covered the phone and gave her a wry grin. "I'm not even going to mention Rita Gomez—this is a small island."

"Ask if I have any mail."

He nodded and said into the phone, "Yes, Jan . . . well, okay. I guess there was just some kind of mix-up. When will you have something? . . . That bad, hm? Or good, I guess if you're in the hotel business. Has any mail come in for Miss Moore?"

Two letters had come in. They would hold them.

Sara said she would pick them up.

"Do you have a car?"

"No, but I can rent one."

"Rental cars are apt to be as scarce as hotel rooms when the island is this jammed. And this is a weekend. I'll drive you."

She felt she should protest a little. "It's several miles down there."

"Sure is. Several beautiful miles and I'm ready for an afternoon off. I'd like to take you—it's one way of repaying Baltimore. I've got a mobile radio in my car—the hospital will beep me if they want to, and there's no wife to beep me. So—all right?"

"All right."

"And then if you don't have other plans for this afternoon I'll take you somewhere else. There will be mobs of people, blood kin, calabash kin, but no tourists. Ever been to a real luau?"

"Never."

"This is a baby luau, but it's a real one. It's for my sister's little Noelani. She's one year old."

(*And then,* she said to the book club, *this very nice little doctor asked me if I'd like to go to a baby luau.*)

The little doctor stood up. He was a head taller than she was and, without his white coat, hard-muscled and lean. Sara got to her feet. She said to the book club absolutely nothing. Woodsriver seemed very far away.

They got into his yellow Jeep and drove down to the Aloha Nui on the Napili coast. It hardly mattered that somebody had picked up her mail a little while before. Rita Gomez hardly mattered. Sara knew that a big question mark hung over the rest of her fifteen days, but she didn't worry about that either.

They bought cheese crackers and Cokes at a filling station and drove on up the coast to a wild spot where waves broke on the rocks in a flow as ceaseless as their words. David told Sara about one of his Hawaiian forebears who had been a *kahuna lapaau,* a doctor skilled in diagnosis and the use of healing herbs. "They had no books, of course, and had to serve an apprenticeship of fifteen years. Some of them were so good at what we now call psychosomatic medicine that the early white men considered them sorcerers. From all I've heard about my great-great-grandfather, he may have cast a spell or two."

Sara could believe it. "Have you always wanted to be a doctor?"

"Ever since I was a little kid. Talk about yourself now. What did you always want to be?"

"Well, I was never really with it. All the rest of the little girls wanted to be something sensible—like a model or a movie star. I used to say I wanted to be a lady with a baby."

He poured more Coke into her cup, laughing.

"So now they're all ladies with babies."

"And you are—don't tell me, a model or a movie star—"

Sara told him about her job at the nursery school and about the old people at the Home, and about her parents, and even about having been in the hospital in the spring. But she told him nothing about the way she had felt then because she had forgotten now that there ever had been a time when she hadn't cared much about living.

The Jeep gave them a bouncy ride over the unimproved road that took them up, down, and around the wildly scenic top of the island. Sheer cliffs made heart-stopping drops to the sea on their left. The few people who lived here were almost all pure Hawaiians; they came rushing out of their tiny houses at the sound of the car, smiling and waving and calling alohas.

Guests had started gathering by the time they reached David's sister's house on the slope above the town of Wailuku. Long tables waited under a temporary thatched structure on the broad front lawn. Flowers wound around the supporting poles and cascaded in showers from the palm-leaf ceiling.

Bemused, Sara was not sure which one of David's young nieces placed a plumeria lei around her shoulders. She sat beside him at a long table whose brown paper covering was almost hidden under fern fronds; mounded in the center was a florist's fortune in orchids, anthuriums and birds-of-paradise. Dogs moved over her feet. The young mother gave her giggly baby girl the first taste of food from a special dish. Sips of a savage drink called *okolehao* made a medley of the laughter and guitars and cries of babies.

"Try this—it's *lomi-lomi,* salmon mixed with tomatoes and green onions . . . Eat the *kalua* pig with your fingers—it's been cooked for hours in a pit with hot stones in its belly . . . Try the poi— don't dare let us hear you say it tastes like library paste, *haole* girl . . . Take some of the chicken on your rice—it's cooked with taro tops and coconut cream . . . No more *okolehao?* . . . Surely some pineapple pie . . ."

The friendly faces were all so richly hued, even the face of the Swedish wife of one of David's brothers. But one face was dominant, that of David's widowed mother. She was a full-blooded Hawaiian. Under creamy-white hair, her skin was like soft beige leather, sagging a little now over bones that once must have given it beauty. The dark eyes were calm, speculative, as they rested from time to time on her son's *haole* guest.

When they had finished eating, the paper with the fern fronds was rolled back with all the scraps, revealing another fresh layer of ferns and paper for the second table. They moved back to sit while an old *tutu,* grandmother, announced that she would perform the ancient hula in honor of the guest Kalai.

"Kalai?"

David was smiling at her. "It's Hawaiian for Sara. I asked her to do it."

In her shapeless cotton dress the old woman moved with dignity, hips swaying in figure eights, shoulders motionless, feet keeping time as her hands wove patterns to the *bom-bom* of a tapa-sided drum. Rain seemed to fall on the thirsty ground; flowers seemed to rise and sway. Birds dipped, sipped nectar, flew; fire burned and the smoke mounted to drift with clouds; a star fell to earth; prayers sighed upward to the winds of heaven.

Sara went forward to embrace her. The word *mahalo* came to her lips as easily as the tears to her eyes.

More hulas. Danced now by young girls with flowers in their hair and on their wrists and ankles. Sweetly, frankly sexual as they darted glances at boyfriends who lounged in the shadows. A string band played grass-shack songs and country rock and soul. More cars came, the girls in mini skirts and long skirts and hot pants and blue jeans. The president of the bank where David's brother-in-law worked came with his wife in formal evening attire. More envelopes went into the calabash. Happy birthday to one-year-old Noelani, who fussed now and was carried off to bed.

David touched the lei around Sara's shoulders, arranging it, lifting her hair and letting his fingers lie against her neck. "They've got several more layers of paper and ferns on those tables, so this goes on half the night. There is a place I want you to see, a picnic spot up in back of the house away from all this. You can look down on the lights of Wailuku."

They scarcely glanced at the lights of Wailuku before they kissed. He drew her close against him and they kissed again and again. She was stunned by the immensity of her feeling for him.

He held her away and looked down at her, smiling a little. She brought her hands down over his hair, feeling the cowlicks rough against her palms.

He said, "I looked at you and I knew—"

The words were an echo, shattering the magic that had been between them. She forced a laugh and tried to free herself from the grasp of the second man in a week who had seen through to The Girl, who was naked and hungry. It hadn't mattered with Joe Egan, but with David Choy . . . She succeeded in pushing his hands away. "Thank you, Joe Egan, wherever you are."

She started hurrying down the hill, but he caught up with her and drew her around to face him. "Oh, I'll save you the protests, David. And I didn't blame Joe Egan any more than I blame you."

"Who the hell is Joe Egan?"

Sara wanted to cry. She looked away and tried to control her voice. "He was a salesman I met in Honolulu. Married. We played a few games—just word games. Fun, I thought. But something about me gave him the idea I was a first-nighter."

"What made you think I thought that?"

"You said the same words he said. He said he took one look at me and he knew. I am ashamed, embarrassed—"

"Let's let Joe Egan finish his sentences and I'll finish mine." His jaws were square in the moonlight and he wasn't smiling. "I looked at you and I knew that I wanted to kiss you. I knew I wanted to get to know you better. I knew I wanted to take you to meet my family—family is very big with us. And that hula . . . Sara, do you think I would want to honor a girl I was planning to take to bed tonight?"

She clung to him and said against his shoulder. "David, I have never felt so awful."

"Good." He lifted her chin and kissed her gently. "Then let's go back to the party and tell everybody goodnight, *haole* girl."

They talked of different things on the way back to the ranch. About one of his patients who was in the Coronary Care Unit at the hospital; he had to check by there tonight and make sure all was going well. About Chris Nielsen. "That kid is their life. When he goes it will destroy them."

"When he—goes?" Sara looked at him quickly. "Do you mean Chris hasn't got long to live?"

He took a little time to reply. "I've been at this business long enough to know that a doctor is a fool to make predictions. But nobody ever thought Chris would make it this long. He's never been well, never had a normal life, never was allowed to run and play like other kids. Of course, he may be better now—I've not seen him since he came back—or his parents may have decided to stop the foolishness of going to one miracle worker after another all over the world. Whatever, I think it's good that they've brought him back where he's happiest. Be nice to him if you get a chance."

They talked a little more about Rita. As they drove between the tiki gods at the ranch entrance David said, "I wouldn't feel right about bringing you back here now if she hadn't been kicked out this morning, but I see no reason why you shouldn't stay on for a while. I'll try to see Mr. Nielsen the first part of the week. You can't continue this trip with Rita, of course."

"No, I couldn't possibly."

He said that he would call her in the morning when he finished rounds, sometime after eleven. He had promised to cover in the afternoon for one of the doctors who had a golf match, but there was a chance he could get somebody else. Would she like to go up to see the crater if he was free?

"It doesn't make any difference what we see. It's your island, David, and I've not seen all of it yet."

"You will. If I can't get the afternoon off, I should be free by seven."

At the louvered door he kissed her goodnight. And then he passed his hands down over her lightly and chuckled.

She tilted her head. "So—?"

"Ah, you funny, skinny little girl you, I'm trying to imagine you pregnant."

Sara was a little breathless as she hurried along the dark hall. She was glad the Saab had not been parked outside because right now she was not sure she could have talked very sensibly to Monte Rivers.

One light burned in the living room. It was dim, but she could see that someone had eaten. She thought about Rita as she looked about, half expecting to find a message with instructions for getting in touch. She wondered if they would have any further contact. How astounding everything was, how puzzling. She thought about Chris, hoping she would see him again.

Sara's room upstairs was dim and sweet with moonlight. A cool breeze caused the white curtains to billow softly, the leaves on the old tree to whisper. She did not turn on the light, and when she went to the window she saw the lights of the Jeep disappearing down the lane. It was only ten o'clock, but she was too keyed up to think of sleep.

Her father's words softly spoken that night on the front porch came through to her now loud and clear: *When it hits you, you'll know it.*

Pop, it has hit me and I know it.

She remembered her mother's wise insistence that she get away from Woodsriver. Not for a moment did she doubt their approval if, please God, she should need it. In spite of the thousands of miles between them, she had never felt closer to her parents than at this moment.

She went over all the words David had said, even the silly ones just before leaving. That could mean nothing. Or that his mind had taken a giant step? No, he probably wasn't as big a fool as she was. She only hoped that as he drove away from her now he wasn't having second thoughts about the *haole* who had thrown herself so readily into his arms. Tomorrow it might be wise to go a little more slowly. If she could.

That fire down there to the right must be a big cane field burning. Far out on the ocean it seemed as if she could see the lights of a ship, though it might be only the waves reflecting the stars; there were millions of them blinking.

And that reminded her. Sara went to the window that looked out on the mountain. She could see a light in the direction of the observatory. Chris had told her he went out there every night.

Be nice to him, David had said.

CHAPTER FIFTEEN

Chris had the dismantled parts of his telescope strewn on a table in the little shack. Sara sat on a chair and he launched into an explanation of his difficulties, using only occasional words she could understand. "The Questar is supposed to be foolproof—but I fooled with it. I loused up the slow-motion control knob." Yellowed star charts were on the walls, meaningless to her.

He wore shorts and a short-sleeved shirt. His long arms and legs were no bigger around than her own. But how beautiful his hair is, she thought, its bright-chestnut fullness curling a little over his ears and on the back of his neck. How beautiful his face would have been if those bones had been fleshed out.

"I was on the track of something that looked promising. Just tonight I spotted a comet I couldn't identify. And now this . . ."

Politely Sara said, "I would have liked to look through it. I have never looked through a real telescope."

"You haven't? Oh, it's tremendous. You can see the rings of Saturn and the moons of Jupiter."

"Can you see the same stars we see over Illinois?"

"We can see the Southern Cross—*Newi* is the Hawaiian name—which you can never see. And at one time or another during the year, we can see all the bright stars and the important constellations. During the fall and winter months we can't see *Na Hiku*—that's the Big Dipper, which is really part of Ursa Major, the Greater Bear."

"Oh." No wonder he puts girls off, she thought.

"It's really fascinating the way the 'pointer' stars at the edge of the bowl come into view. I've not been here for the last couple of winters, but in January I always used to look forward to seeing those two stars, *Dubhe* and *Merak,* pointing straight at Polaris."

"That's—pretty interesting. I think."

He grinned. "What would you like to talk about? I'd like to talk about something that's important to you. Do you collect stamps or coins or anything?"

"No, I don't collect anything. Sorry." She doubted if they had anything in common. She wondered, What was it like to know you were going to die? Or did he know?

"Do you play chess? I have several games going with people all over the world—Rome, Tokyo—"

"No. And I've never traveled. That's why I'm so thrilled to have this trip."

"You said you had won a contest?"

"Yes. It was sponsored by one of your father's companies. How come you don't know anything about your father's business?"

"I just don't care about it. He's given up trying to get me interested. But I'm glad you won. It could have been some fat old schoolteacher prowling around out there this morning. Want to know something?—I never thought I saw a honeycreeper."

"You didn't?"

"No. Crested honeycreepers never come down below three thousand feet. It was just an excuse to talk to you. I'm more interested in girls than in honeycreepers."

Impulsively she put out her hand and touched his hand and it was so cold it was like touching the hand of somebody who was already dead. His bony fingers turned and clutched hers as if he was grateful that she would touch him. And then he let go just as suddenly, as if he might have read her mind.

Sara started talking to cover her discomfort and disguise her pity, hoping she made sense. "I met your mother this morning. She was so nice to me. We talked for a while and she showed me some of her things in the cases."

"My mother liked you. She told me you were from some little town in Illinois."

"Yes. Woodsriver."

"What is it like?"

"We-e-ll, aside from the fact that the woods are all gone and the river is a mile away there isn't anything very interesting to tell."

"What do the kids do for excitement in a town like that?"

"There isn't any excitement unless they make it. There's one movie. They have dates and ride around in cars. Swim in the summer and play tennis. Ice-skate in the winter." His face had a wistful look and she stopped, knowing she was talking about things he could never hope to do. Just sitting here, the sound of his breathing was labored.

He said matter-of-factly as if he read her mind again and didn't want her pity, "I've never been allowed to do anything much because of . . ."—his fist gave a knock against his chest as if he hated it—"but I went to a whorehouse once."

"You—did?"

"Are you shocked?"

"Well, no, but—" Flabbergasted might have been the word.

"I've been wanting to tell somebody for the longest time, but there never has been anybody I could tell."

She couldn't think of anything to say.

"You know the thought I had? I thought, what if I died there? It was in Paris. The girl was kind of old. She was nice to me, but—well, she sure as hell wasn't worth dying for. Her eyes were all painted blue with white streaks. Like a parrot. She chewed spearmint gum and stuck it on the headboard. There were some other wads of gum on the headboard. I haven't been able to stand the smell of spearmint gum ever since." He made a sound almost like laughter, a little hoarse. "That was when I was nineteen. I was—you know—a little healthier then."

Sara wanted to put her arms around him and hold him close. She could not bear the thought of his dying when he'd had only that one whorehouse girl. She wanted to murmur to him and tell him she loved him. And in a way, she truly did. As if he had been a young brother she yearned over, mourned for. Tears came to her eyes and she hoped he wouldn't notice them, but he was holding a knob in his hands, turning it, examining it.

"I've been sick my whole goddamn life. I've been a guinea pig. Every time my mother reads about something new, we go and I have it. Only, no more, Sara. To hell with the tube in the throat and the suctioning. I've had it with the big needles and the little knives and the oxygen tents and the doctors sometimes with blood still on their coats."

He put back his head and said between his teeth, "All the bastards in the teaching hospitals come around in packs and stare at you." A small scar she had not noticed before was just below his

Adam's apple. "You see pictures, horrible obscene pictures of your insides, and they tell you what they have done, or what they are going to do, or what they are sorry they can't do. And you learn words, horrible obscene words you wish you didn't know."

"I was in a hospital for five weeks this spring, Chris, and I learned some words too. They really can dream up some pretty gruesome things to do. I'm sure I didn't have to go through what you did, but I know a little what it's like."

"What was wrong with you?"

"Nothing. They just said I had an unidentified virus and sent me home. For a while there I had made up my mind that I was probably going to die. My symptoms seemed to add up to a fatal illness."

"And—how did you feel when you thought—?"

"Well, I was in kind of a thing along about then and I told myself I didn't much care. Now everything is different." David, she thought. But not just David.

"Good. I bet you're in love with somebody."

"Yes." She got up. If she stayed there any longer she might find herself telling him about David Choy and it wasn't time for that yet. "I'd better go back now. It's getting late."

"I'll walk up with you. I can work on this thing some more in the morning."

Sara paced her steps to his slow ones, noticing that even this gentle slope seemed to make him short of breath. He stopped once to rest and looked at the sky. "The moon is in Ku."

She looked up at the waning moon.

"The old ones believed that when the moon is in Ku the forces of the supernatural hold sway."

"Tell me about some of the old superstitions."

"They weren't all superstitions. Much of what my people believed was true. It gave them comfort to believe in the signs. They liked knowing that there was an intelligence greater than theirs that could see into the future. That a watch was being kept."

The moon-touched trees shook their leaves a little uneasily. The breeze seemed to wait. It was not hard to believe in the supernatural on a night like this.

He looked down at her, as tall as one of the legendary chiefs. "My ancestors had no written language, but they could read the skies and interpret the meaning in the clouds and the rainbow and the way the rains fell. They read the sea and the wind and the thunder and the flight of birds. The appearance of certain kinds of fish meant disaster. And if a flame would not burn they thought it meant death."

"But to believe too much in all those things would be a worry."

He didn't seem to hear her. He put his head back as if listening. "This is the time of the moon and the time of the night when the Great Marching Dead sometimes come."

"The Great—?"

"Yes. The ones who have gone on, the warriors, the chiefs. Sometimes you can feel only a vibration of the earth. Sometimes the noise has been so great it is as if their feet tramped on the roof of our house. I used to hide my head under my pillow for fear I would see them, but my mother always heard them too— not everybody can—and she would come and hold me. She told me that they would never harm me because I was one of theirs. Even if I looked at their faces the *aumakua,* the spirit of my ancestors, would cry, 'No, he is mine!' and I would be safe. So after a while I was never afraid."

"And did you ever see them?"

"No. I would like to. I have heard the drums and the nose flutes. Sara, do you believe me?"

"Yes." At that moment she truly did.

They went toward the house. Two cars were parked there, the green Saab and another car she had not seen before.

"Will you come back out there again in the morning, Sara? There is something else I want to show you."

"Yes. I'll try to come early. Goodnight, Chris." She pulled his face down and kissed him. There were so many kinds of love, and on this night she felt under many spells.

CHAPTER SIXTEEN

The long hall was illuminated only by a few cracks of moonlight that quivered through the shutters from the dark garden. Sara hurried, stumbled when she came to the three steps, and when she threw the door open she was almost blinded by the brightness of the kitchen light.

Rita was standing just inside the door as if she had heard her coming.

"Where in the hell have you been"—she flicked her bright smile —"sweetie?"

Sara lifted one shoulder and started to move past her. "Out." It was the "sweetie" that made her mad.

Rita's hand closed over her arm. "Just *out*? Monte and I just got back from combing this whole island in separate cars. I thought something dreadful had happened. I didn't dare tell Mr. Nielsen that our little friend had dropped from sight without the courtesy of a single word."

Sara wasn't much interested in hearing Rita talk about courtesy. She pulled away from Rita's hand and met the big dark eyes. "I thought Mrs. Nielsen told you not to come back."

"I don't have to prostrate myself every time the royal chamber-pot is carried past. Her Majesty's little whims don't bother me at all. When Mr. Nielsen fires me that will be something else." She gestured toward the living room. "Come, sweetie, I want you to meet our friend Monte Rivers."

Sara had not seen him. He was standing back in the shadows by the fireplace. He could have played a priest's role if he'd worn a cassock. His hair was dark and his eyes somber. Or he could have been a dancer, she thought, as he moved gracefully toward her in rather tight black pants and jersey and murmured something that could have been How do you do?

"Miss Moore must have found herself a boyfriend, I think, to squire her around the island." His face was without expression and so was his voice.

"Yes," said Sara.

"Our shy, sweet little Sara?" Rita was smiling at her warmly. "Well, well. How terribly nice for you, Sara. Who was it?"

"A friend of a friend."

"What's his name?"

Sara looked down at the table, tapping her fingers beside the overflowing ashtray. *David Choy, who examined your battered child*. She might say that later if the time should come when she was ready for a big scene. On a crumpled cigarette pack she read a name. "His name is Reynolds."

"Oh. Splendid. And what did you and this Mr. Reynolds do?"

"We went to a baby luau."

"What did they do?" asked Monte Rivers. "Cook a baby?"

"A pig, Monte," said Rita. "A baby luau is *for* a baby. A charming little mindless holdover from God knows when. The money envelopes in the calabash pay for the whole bash. Perfectly harmless if you go in for the simple joys. Whose luau was it?"

"I didn't catch the name," said Sara. "I think I will go on up to bed."

Monte Rivers said, "Just a minute. Did you eat any of the pork?"

"Of course. It was delicious."

"Trichinosis is a very interesting disease. Millions of little worms invade all the tissues of the body. Fascinating. There isn't any cure for a bad case of trichinosis—and that's what you can get when you eat pork that hasn't been properly cooked."

"Oh, come off it, Monte," said Rita. "Don't be so superior. The pig is cooked for hours. We're not quite savages."

"I am just thinking about her health. She could have ptomaine by bedtime. She could have salmonella, botulism. The simple, harmless little pastime could—"

"Monte, hush. My goodness, you'll scare the child." Rita smiled at him and then at Sara. "You have a letter."

"Oh." Sara had forgotten completely about her mail. "*A* letter? They said—"

"*They* said . . . ? That reminds me—you did a bit of checking up, didn't you, Sara? When Monte very thoughtfully went all the way down there for your mail they told him that somebody had been checking up to see if it was really true about there being no reservations. Why in the world would I bother making that up? The reservations had been made a long time ago, as I told you the first time we talked on the phone. Naturally, they were in the name of the person who was originally scheduled to have this trip. You had forgotten that, I guess, hadn't you?"

Sara felt the color come up in her cheeks. "But they did say that there were two letters for me."

"They were wrong. They made a mistake." Rita went to the mantel and picked up a letter. "There is only one."

Sara took the letter without saying any more and went up the stairs. When she reached the top she heard Monte Rivers say something in a language she didn't understand.

The letter was from her parents and had been written before the telephone call. "We miss you . . . We love you . . . Take good care of yourself . . . We move the pins on the map . . ."

Rita came up. "Sweetie, I'm going now. I borrowed a friend's car and promised to return it tonight." She came and patted Sara's shoulder. "I guess I was a little bit snotty to you down there tonight. I'm sorry. But I was so worried about you! I want us to go right on being good friends."

Sara looked away. "What did Monte Rivers say to you just now as I came upstairs? In Spanish or whatever?"

"Portuguese. He lived in Brazil at one time. I don't understand it very well—nor does he speak it very well. Something about what pretty legs you have."

"I am not a bit crazy about staying out here alone with him like this."

"Oh, you silly little thing." She looked amused. "You're really not his type, you know."

Sara's eyes went to the door. "I can't even lock the door—there isn't any key."

"This island has always been such a safe place that people haven't bothered with keys much. And out here there is nothing whatever to worry about. You can push the chest across the door if you're worried. And then you'll at least wake up and scream your head off if anybody tries to get in."

"Way out here so far from the main part of the house I could probably do just that without anybody hearing me."

"Nonsense. Now, in the morning what do you think you would like to do?"

"Nothing."

"I'll buy that—you mean sleep till noon or so? Maybe we can do something fun then in the afternoon. I expect Monte will want to sleep late too and he can bring you in. Isn't there any special thing you would like to do?"

"No." Sara wasn't ready to let Rita know anything. By noon David would have called. She didn't intend to see Rita tomorrow at all or to stay here another night either.

"We'll talk about it tomorrow. Nighty-night. Sleep tight. And don't you worry your pretty head about anything."

Sara was sitting at the dressing table taking her make-up off when she heard the murmur of voices below the window. The car started up and Monte raised his voice. "Why not? Since you don't seem to be particularly welcome here, I think you should be the one to go see the Bird People."

The *Bird People?* That made no sense. The car drove away and Sara heard Monte come back in the house and go to his room.

She wasn't going to worry about the Bird People, but she did want a key. She remembered having seen one in the kitchen door; there was a chance it might fit. She waited a few minutes and then went downstairs in her bare feet.

She did not turn on a light. No crack of light showed under his bedroom door, but she knew he might not be asleep, so she moved quietly. The floor felt gummy against the soles of her feet, as if it hadn't been washed for years. The kitchen door had not been locked. She took out the key which fit loosely as if it might be a skeleton key.

And apparently it was. After a bit of jiggling she succeeded in turning the lock on her door. She felt better. Although it was late she got out stationery to answer the letter from her parents.

What a poor thing a letter was. How could she make them understand Mrs. Nielsen, so regal in her anger, so wistful in her admission that she prayed to all the gods? "My hostess is descended from missionary stock and Hawaiian nobility. She has been kind to me."

Love at first sight was a silly phrase; instant insanity might best describe her seizure. "I met a very nice young doctor today and he took me to a baby luau in honor of his sister's baby, who is one year old."

Chris might be hardest of all to describe. How could she tell them about the Night Marchers when even now the spell she had been under had dissipated a little? "Chris, the Nielsens' son, has told me a lot about Hawaiian lore . . ."

Sara looked at what she had written. She had not even mentioned the fact that Rita had left, and that now she was staying here with Monte Rivers. Actually, the whole truth about almost any of the things that had happened on this eventful day would have alarmed them. But it had been the best day of her life. Even her brief dismay here this morning had turned into something good.

Monte Rivers was moving around in the living room below; she had thought he was asleep. She smelled smoke. He must be burning something in the fireplace. How odd that he should have remembered something that had to be burned at this hour. She heard a sound as if he replaced the fireplace screen, and then nothing more.

What had he burned? Her other letter? The girl at the hotel had said there were two letters for her. Tomorrow she might take a look through the ashes to see if she could find a scrap that would tell her something. Not that it made very much difference. Nobody was sending her any money. Nobody was writing her love letters.

Sara addressed and stamped her own letter and went to bed. The old tree outside the window rubbed its knuckles against the screen. The whispering leaves seemed almost to say her name.

David. She put her mind on him, the look of his beautifully planed face, the surge of her response to his kisses, the urgent pressure of his lean body against hers.

She hoped that tomorrow she could remember to have some sense, but she planned with a reckless lack of it now. She saw herself beside him, made new, the girl she had never yet been, her face shining with fulfillment. Already she knew how tenderly they would love, and with what abandonment to joy. She saw their children, bright-faced as flowers.

All night Sara dreamed of David Choy.

CHAPTER SEVENTEEN

The kitchen was a mess. Servants to do what had to be done, Rita had said. Sara Moore had washed dishes ever since she could remember without particularly minding; here she hated it. It was so unbelievable to have come from the elegance of the Summer Palace Lodge to this dark excuse for a kitchen and have to clean up a mess left by someone she disliked as much as she disliked Monte Rivers.

When she had brought a little order to the place, she poured a cup of the coffee that she had put on to perk when she first came down. She stood drinking it, most of her annoyance gone. She was glad she was here. Otherwise she would never have had any reason to look up David Choy. She would never have met Chris.

She made a piece of toast, remembering that she had said she would be out there early. She hurried, moving quietly, not wanting

Monte Rivers' door to open before she went out. She didn't even want to have to say good morning to him.

Before she left, she did take time to look in the fireplace. There was nothing but the blackened scraps of what might have been a letter, though not necessarily a letter to her. There were a number of perplexing little things she could have worried about, but she had better things to do. She washed the ashes from her hands and went on out.

Chris must have heard her coming along the path, for he was standing outside the shack waiting for her. The thinness that had been so cruelly apparent last night was covered somewhat by what he wore, white slacks, and a long-sleeved shirt with a turtleneck that covered the scar she had seen on his throat.

"I never really believed you'd come so early."

"I guess I'm not used to the time change yet."

"I'm going to show you something that nobody else knows about yet. Do you know what a lava tube is?"

"No."

He gestured toward the mountain. "Haleakala is a dormant volcano. It's been inactive since before the white man came, although it can't really be said to be extinct. At the time of the eruptions—no one knows how many—some of the molten lava was forced through the sides of the mountain, forming tubes that hardened after the lava had made its way to the sea."

His sometimes stilted way of talking, Sara realized, was typical of a person who has lived half his life in books.

"There are said to be hundreds of lava tubes on Maui. Many of them, I suppose, are still unknown. But in the old days some of them were used as burial caves for the dead."

"And you mean some of the bodies may still be there?"

"Usually only the bones. The flesh was stripped from the bones before burial."

"Chris Nielsen!" Sara shivered in the warm sunlight.

"Don't you want to hear about it?"

"I suppose so. It's such a ghoulish thought."

"Maybe not to them. I suppose there were all sorts of religious ceremonies and rites that saw them through it. Anyhow, the bones were wrapped in tapa and hidden by the priests. They had to be hidden to keep them from being stolen and used."

"*Used?*" She gave him another squeamish look.

"Used. The bones, especially the bones of a chief, were thought to possess a particular power, *mana*. They used the long bones for tools and weapons. The collarbones were especially suited for fishhooks. Enemies would sometimes even use the skulls for spittoons, and this was a special disgrace not only to the dead man but to all the members of his family and his descendants."

They had started walking slowly over the uneven ground, not following a path. He stopped to rest. "I suppose you've guessed it— I've found a burial cave."

His thin face was shining and his smoked-silver eyes burned with excitement. "I've not told anyone else about it. It would get in the papers. The museum people would want to come—and they must, of course, because the owners of the land must share a thing like this. But not yet. My mother will hate all the fuss and publicity, and right now isn't the time for it."

"How come nobody has ever found it before?"

"A big storm hit the island last year when we were away. It caused some landslides. When I first got back I noticed that this part of the slope had a different look. I never thought very much about it until one day last week when I happened to be looking through my binoculars. I saw then that there seemed to be a narrow opening in the side of the mountain over there. It's not far away, so of course I had to go for a closer look. I don't think anybody else knows about it."

"What about the caretaker?"

"No, he would have mentioned it. But even if he had found it he would never have dared go in. He's Island-born, and he would know about the curse that's supposed to be on those who desecrate the place of the dead."

"The curse—?"

"I don't desecrate, Sara. I haven't touched anything. I go there as a scientist would go. I have a right to be there. My family has owned this land for generations and I am sure some of my ancestors are buried there. Do you want to see it?"

(At home, her mother and father would have come from church and eaten their Sunday dinner. Her father about now would be settling himself to read the Chicago *Tribune*. Her mother would be washing dishes, and no doubt from time to time her eyes would go to the pin on the map that said Sara was staying at the Aloha Nui.)

"I want to see it, Chris."

"Come on, then. Watch out for the thorns on the wild lantana."

A tree had fallen a couple of hundred yards from the shack, its roots lifting a lid of earth that revealed, but just barely, an opening in the hillside. They crowded past the roots and dirt through a narrow fissure. Immediately they were in almost total darkness.

Chris put his hand out to a flashlight that lay in a little niche. "I keep this here. Come on. You have to stoop low for a few feet." He extended one hand behind him and Sara caught hold of it.

When they were able to stand upright, the flashlight beam showed that they were in a kind of tunnel. It was thick with the smell of ancient dust and a peculiar mustiness that she couldn't identify. Water dripped somewhere, making a sound that was unnaturally loud as they stood quietly for a few seconds looking about them.

"Come on," said Chris, his voice echoing.

She followed him. He directed the light to a ledge that looked as if it had been hacked out of one side of the wall. Bundles were stacked there, different as to size and shape, wrapped in tapa. In a hushed tone Sara said, "When you came in here you were probably the first in—how long, Chris?"

"Perhaps two hundred years. The museum people will tell us that. See how neat everything is. Look at the mats and all those calabashes. I don't think this cave has ever been looted the way some of these places have been."

"I should think the idea of a curse would stop most people."

"There is also a legend that says anyone who is in a burial cave at certain sacred hours must run for his life before he is overtaken by the terrible cold that comes before the dead begin their marching."

Sara could tell by the way he spoke that he probably believed it. She did not, but she was ready to go back into the sunlight. "It's fascinating, Chris. Let's go."

"No, there are some other things I want you to see."

Reluctantly she followed him a little further. He flashed the light onto a smooth portion of the wall, where she saw crude figures and symbols. Some of them looked like the designs she had seen on tapa; others resembled what the nursery-school children produced when told to draw a man. Some kind of animal, perhaps a boar, was represented with a tusk.

He moved the light again so that she could see far back into the cave. "Now, back there is a chimney sort of thing. I think it may lead to another burial cave above, maybe a more important one. A person could climb up there, I think. I haven't tried it, too risky all alone. I don't suppose you—"

"You suppose right." She said it firmly.

"There might even be feather cloaks up there, and the old canoes that the legends tell about. Sometimes whole bodies have been found, fairly well preserved, with tattoos."

Sara laughed a little. She took hold of the hand that held the flashlight and directed it back toward the mouth of the cave. "Your ancestors may be buried here, Chris, but mine are not. And if the chiefs were to start walking they would not say I was one of theirs. Come *on*."

They stooped again to go under the low bridge of rock. When Chris put the flashlight back in its niche he grinned at her. "You were scared."

"Not really. Well, a little. Let's just say I have a healthy respect for the dead."

Outside in the welcome warmth of the sun they sat under a tree that bloomed with fragrant golden flowers. Chris leaned against the trunk and closed his eyes as if very tired. Sara shook particles of dirt out of her hair. "You've not even told your mother about the cave?"

"No. She would have been afraid for me to prowl around in there alone."

"How long will it be before you want everybody to know?"

"Soon. It has to be soon. Before I go."

There was no mistaking what he meant. She said faintly, "Chris—"

"It's in the stars. *Que sera, sera,* Sara, and all that. I dreamed last night that a calabash was broken. That means bad luck hovers near. In the old times a calabash held everything—food, clothing, all one's possessions. It held one's life. In my dream I saw my mother crying and picking up the pieces. I knew she was trying to put the pieces of my life back together. There was no way."

"Well, now look, Chris. It's not sensible to let yourself be upset by a silly dream."

"I'm not upset. I just know. And I dream of the sea. That's supposed to mean—"

Sara interrupted. "My father had a dream about me before I left. If I had let myself be upset by it I wouldn't be here under this tree talking to you now."

"What did he dream?"

"He dreamed about me being in the hospital—and that was a dream about something that was past. Maybe at the time he hadn't let himself admit his fears about it. In your conscious mind, Chris, you know it's bad luck to dream about a broken calabash. So your subconscious dreaming mind takes over and presents you with this fear that you don't acknowledge in the daytime."

"But I do acknowledge it in the daytime. Only it's not fear any more. I've accepted it. Nothing more can be done. God, no more knives. I was relieved when they told my parents that in St. Louis."

"St. Louis? What hospital were you in?"

"Brill."

"I was at Brill. I went the first week in April and stayed five weeks."

"I was there then. I went in the middle of April and stayed three weeks."

They stared at each other. They laughed a little. Chris said, "Why, that's uncanny."

"Isn't it? What a small world. I can't believe it. Say, did you happen to know a Dr. Durham?"

"I don't remember. There have been so many that I don't even listen to their names any more. I hate doctors."

"What about David Choy—you know him, don't you?"

"Oh, sure. He's different. He's a swell guy. How come you know David?"

"I happened to meet him yesterday." She glanced at her watch and saw that it was getting on toward eleven. "I want to ask you something quickly and then I've got to go—who are the Bird People?"

"The—Bird People? I don't know. Why would you think I'd know?"

"It just sounds like your kind of thing."

"You mean—kind of weird?" He pulled a handful of grass and threw it at her, laughing.

"No, no, of course not." She wondered how much he knew about Rita Gomez, but decided she had better not get into that sordid story. She scrambled to her feet. "Chris, we'll have to talk some more about it, and about Brill Hospital—that's fantastic. But you stay here now and I'll run on back. David is going to call me sometime after eleven."

"You said last night you were in love. I figured it was some-body at home, but—"

"There's nobody at home." She leaned to put a quick kiss on his forehead, and then hurried toward the house.

CHAPTER EIGHTEEN

Monte Rivers was eating his breakfast at a card table in the living room when Sara came in. "I thought you were going to sleep until noon. Where have you been?" He hadn't shaved; she had seen movies of Marlon Brando looking like that.

"Out." The kitchen was cluttered again. She took a water jug out of the refrigerator and poured some water into a glass.

"Doing what all this time?"

"Just looking around."

"What were you looking for?"

He would be the last person she'd ever tell about the burial cave. "Oh, nothing special. Rita told me that there is an old *heiau* up there somewhere."

"A—what?"

"The remains of a temple."

"A temple. I have to laugh. The way these people blat all the time about their ancient religion and their culture. I notice they don't have much to say about the poor son of a bitch who discovered these islands. The ignorant natives thought Captain Cook was a god, and when they discovered he wasn't, they killed him and made fly swatters out of the palms of his hands."

Sara went through the living room. "Has there been a telephone call for me?" It was not quite eleven yet.

"No. Who would be calling?"

What possible business was it of his? She started to go up to her room. "My friend might call." For the moment she couldn't remember the name she had read off that cigarette package last night when she had been so annoyed by Rita's prying. As she was annoyed now by his.

"*Mr.* Reynolds, you mean?"

"Yes."

"What's his first name?"

She could not remember that she had ever disliked anyone so much before. "Rudolph."

"We are going out, so get ready."

From halfway up the stairs she looked down at him. "I am going to wait here for my friend to call."

"Twelve o'clock is when I'm planning to leave."

"Fine. You just go on without me."

He gave her a look and went into his room.

Sara washed her hair in her splintery little bathroom. She kept turning off the water to listen, afraid she might miss her summons to the phone. Again she wondered whether Monte Rivers had a phone in his room, and then realized that if he were to be of any use to the Nielsens in possible medical emergencies he'd have to have one. Very likely he'd have a separate line with separate listing, which would mean that David's call would come to the main part of the house. She hoped that would be the case so she wouldn't have to go into Monte's bedroom to take the call.

For the next hour she sat in her sunny window drying her long hair, the door open so she could be sure to hear that first knock on the kitchen door. There could be many reasons why David was late in calling her. He could have had an emergency. Or maybe the telephone in the other part of the house had been in use. Yes, that was logical, Mr. Nielsen with all his business interests. She was not particularly concerned.

She thought about Chris and the odd coincidence of their having been in St. Louis at the same time and now meeting here. Chris would probably say it was in the stars, or maybe, with his Calvinist ancestors, that it was predestined. Whatever strange chance had brought them together, she would always be glad she had the chance to know him. And as for David . . .

Monte Rivers called upstairs. "I'm ready to leave."

Sara pulled on the robe that lay ready and went part of the way down the stairs. It was a little amusing to see that he was wearing a brilliantly patterned aloha shirt, since he pretended to take such a dim view of the Islands.

"How come you aren't ready to go?"

"I'm not going out."

"What are you going to do all day, just hang around here and wait for your boyfriend to call?"

"He will call. Don't you worry about it. You go ahead."

He got out a cigarette and snapped his lighter on angrily. "Rita is waiting. She was planning to take you somewhere. After all, this is a vacation trip and you should be making the most of it. What about lunch?"

"I'll find something here. I saw some cans." Call or no call, food or no food, Sara had no intention of ever being seen anywhere on this island with Rita Gomez again.

"That's ridiculous. Come on. Hurry up and get into your clothes. Rita won't like it if you're late."

"Late? Didn't you hear what I said? I am not going out with you at all."

He went into his room and slammed the door.

Sara frowned and looked toward the slammed door. What was this anyhow? Why didn't he want to go without her? Rita might have some reason to think she was responsible for her, but Monte Rivers certainly didn't. He didn't like her, it was obvious, any better than she liked him.

She lay on her bed. It had been the luckiest break of her life to have the chance to come here, but now she couldn't wait to get away. When David called she would tell him she didn't care what sort of place he could find for her—third rate, fourth rate, anything at all would do.

She hadn't mentioned Monte Rivers to David, nor had she then even met Monte. She was sure that when David found out about this cozy setup he would agree that staying here was impossible.

She found a paperback that she had bought in the Los Angeles airport and read two or three chapters. It was getting very warm in the room. She was aware of drowsiness. She didn't want to sleep, but she'd had only five or six hours of sleep last night and a little nap might be a good idea since she was sure she'd be going out tonight. She knew she would waken at once at the sound of a knock.

The light in the room had changed when she awoke. For a moment she was disoriented. She had been dreaming that she was at home and that Brenda Jean Benson was scratching at the back screen door trying to get in. It was only the old tree. When she looked at her watch she jumped out of bed, not believing that it could possibly be after six. She pulled on a dress quickly and went downstairs.

She had expected that Monte Rivers would have left, but he was playing solitaire at the little table. He glanced up. "Were you asleep?"

"Yes."

"Your face is flushed as if you have a fever."

"It was hot up there. Did I have a call?"

"No." He looked down at his cards.

Sara went through the kitchen door and hurried along the corridor.

"Where are you going?"

She didn't answer, fumbling a little with the latch of the door into the dim garden.

He caught up with her on the other side of the door. "What the hell do you think you're going to do? You haven't any business coming in here."

She struck at the hand on her arm. "Let go of me!"

A voice said, "What is the trouble?"

The tall figure of Mr. Nielsen had risen from the chair where Sara first had seen him. He took a few steps toward them, a glass in his hand. It was difficult to see through the shrubbery to the shadowed lanai, but he seemed to be alone.

"Has there been a call for me, Mr. Nielsen?"

"No."

Monte Rivers said, "Everything is all right, Mr. Nielsen."

The tall man's eyes were on Sara. "Is everything all right?"

"Yes." She wanted to say that Dr. Choy would be in touch with him, but while she hesitated Mr. Nielsen turned abruptly as he had done that other time and went into the house. His steps were unsteady.

Sara went back in, with Monte Rivers just behind her.

He said, "You didn't believe me, did you?"

She didn't answer. She had a shaky feeling, as if she might start crying. Her head ached. She sat in one of the chairs by the fireplace. Maybe David hadn't called. Maybe there had been some reason why he simply couldn't call. But he had said that even if he couldn't get the afternoon off he would be free by seven. She had no intention of moving away from this spot where she could see that kitchen door. It would be Mei-ling or Kimo, most likely, who would come with the message.

Monte Rivers had stopped in the kitchen to fix himself a drink. "You had better eat something. I opened a can of ham. There's some bread for sandwiches."

"No thanks, I'm not hungry."

He came in and seated himself at the card table again. "You look sick to me."

I am sick, she thought. I'm sick with wondering why David hasn't called. I'm sick at the thought of maybe having to spend another night in this place. But I'll get well fast enough when I hear that knock on the door.

"You'll not see Rita tomorrow."

"Good."

"What's the matter, don't you like Rita either?"

"No."

"She's going to Honolulu to get the respirator fixed. She must have dropped the goddamned thing or something."

"The what?" Not that she cared.

He waited a minute, dealing cards. "Oh, they have to have this thing on their plane for the kid. He has trouble breathing sometimes. Why don't you go and fix yourself a drink instead of sitting on the edge of that chair waiting for your boyfriend to call?"

She hated him so much that her head pounded. She reached for a book on the shelf beside her without looking at the title. After she had turned the pages for a while she saw that it was titled *The Story of Hawaiian Pineapple: 1890–1926.*

From time to time she could tell that Monte Rivers looked at her. She wondered if he could read the title of her book from there and if he might be smiling a little. She couldn't remember that she had seen him smile. She turned pages, her ears tuned to the steps that she willed to come along the dark passage out there

"Better fix yourself a drink." He got up to replenish his own. "I can pour one for you if you like."

Cheers. Everything was getting a little too chummy. She got up and went upstairs.

Darkness was descending suddenly the way it seemed always to do here. Sara sat at a window, away from the one with the nudging branches, and looked at the southwestern sky, where the sun was just finishing its nightly performance. From here she could see past the house and here and there catch a glimpse of the long driveway.

Her mind presented her with a forlorn hope: the phone might be out of order and David might give up on it finally and drive out here. She could see the lights, recognize that yellow Jeep at the first glance. He knew which door to come to. When it parked below she would lean and say, "David, I'm here. I'll be right down."

Her nails cut her palms. Was she some kind of fool to be expecting him to come after all this time? He had had hours to reflect, and perhaps she should do some reflecting too, sensible for a change.

What did she know of this culture he was part of? Were standards higher than in the ones at home that had taken such a beating these last years? Family is very big with us, he had said. Had David Choy decided that he didn't want to honor a girl who had kissed him with such passion, admitting she had gone out with a married man in Honolulu? For all her pretty protests, hadn't her actions perhaps drowned out her words?

Her face burned so in the darkness that it seemed she really must have a fever. She walked around the room. Me and eager Eloise. Two of a kind. Desperate. She had laughed at poor Eloise. Laugh now at Sara.

No, not now. Years from now maybe.

No, never.

As she had done so many times in the last hours, Sara went over his words, trying to take some crumb of hope. They had thrilled her then, but now she read them differently. For *I'm trying to imagine you pregnant* read: *The way you go around kissing people you've just met, you're asking for it.*

David was not going to call. He was not going to come. Her head was killing her. She wished she had some aspirin, but she had not brought any because she never had headaches. She would not go downstairs to look in the medicine cabinet. She would not ask Monte Rivers if he had any.

She drank some water, splashed it over her face, then locked her door, glad she had the key whether she was his type or not. She went to bed.

She had slept for hours this afternoon and now sleep would not come. The tree scraped at the screen as if it would wear a hole in it. Her throat seemed to be getting sore. She kept swallowing to see how bad it was. Hours went by. Strange images floated and she believed she might be a little delirious.

Is this the girl? Yes, this is the girl. She hasn't a chance. She had dreamed the words, but they woke her. She sat up in bed her heart pounding, very frightened. A crazy thought came from nowhere. What if she really did have some awful disease and nobody had told her? And what if some very rich person, feeling sorry for someone who had to die so young, had arranged all this to make it seem as if she had won a contest?

Somebody very, very rich. Like Mr. Nielsen.

Her thoughts fell over each other. Chris had been at the hospital then too and Mr. Nielsen had probably been there also part of the time. Maybe that was why Mr. Nielsen's eyes were so sad when they looked at her. Maybe that was why Rita had been so solicitous for her health. Why, even Monte Rivers had seemed to care that she had a fever.

The whispering noise filled the room. Damn that tree! How could she ever sleep with that thing scraping away like that? As if to say, Notice me, come close to me. Like that senile old man at the Home. A trick of the moonlight turned the shaky branches into a face with a mouth open in a silent scream.

Would it never be morning? Oh, in the morning she was really going to get out of here!

But in the morning she was very ill.

CHAPTER NINETEEN

From below, Monte Rivers' voice. "You up there. Aren't you going to get up?"

"I'm sick."

He came upstairs and turned the knob, rattling it impatiently. "Oh, come on, let me in."

Sara pulled on her robe and unlocked the door, then fell back into bed, pulling the covers and bedspread up over her. She had been alternately freezing and burning up all night, and now her teeth chattered with chill.

"It's no wonder to me that you're sick. Anybody who would go to some dirty, filthy native hovel and eat—"

She whispered, "It wasn't a dirty, filthy hovel."

"Okay, okay. What's wrong with you?"

"My throat."

"Let me see."

"It's just sore."

"Well, you can let me take a look at it, can't you?"

She hated having him so close. He leaned over and she shut her eyes and opened her mouth. His hand felt cool on her forehead as he turned her head for a better look. She cringed away.

"Well, your throat is a little inflamed, but there aren't any spots. You do have a fever—I thought so last night. When did your throat start getting sore?"

"In the night."

"Do you have pain anywhere—in your chest, your abdomen? What about your glands, your joints?"

She shook her head.

"Rita said you had mentioned being in the hospital this spring. Is this the way you felt then?"

"Sicker then." The thought she'd had in the night came back with a little thrill of fear. Had she really been sicker then or not? Was this the same thing coming back?

She spoke with an effort. "I want you to call a doctor. Dr. David Choy. My doctor gave me his name."

He said a little stiffly, "I have my M.D. Perhaps Rita hasn't told you."

It was on the tip of her tongue to say she wanted a real doctor. Certainly she wanted one who cared enough to go on practicing. "I—yes, she mentioned it. But I'd rather you called Dr. Choy."

He shrugged. "All right, I'll call him. But doctors here don't go chasing all over the island for every tourist who crooks a finger. You're not back at home in your little one-horse town now, you know."

Sara turned her face to her pillow. How she wished she were back in her own blue-walled room with the white wicker furniture, indulged, worried over, deeply loved. Under the circumstances it was humiliating to have to ask a favor of David. He might think she was only faking an excuse to get him to come out here. But she could not, would not, spend another night here, and no matter how David felt about her personally he might be willing to put her in the hospital.

After Monte Rivers had gone downstairs she threw off the covers, burning up. She sat up and leaned to look into the mirror. Her face was shiny red and her eyes bright and sick with fever. Her hair was a tangled mess, and her nightgown was damp and smelled of perspiration. David would almost have to come; he knew about last spring's illness. She must try to take some kind of sponge bath, slip into a clean nightgown and brush her hair.

Sara got out of bed, her head swimming, and went into the bathroom. She would know how David felt about her the minute he walked in the door.

Back in bed, exhausted with her efforts, the thought she'd had in the night came back. A stupid thought now in the light of morning. Dr. Durham had assured her that she was perfectly all right, with nothing to worry about. He wouldn't have lied to her, nor to her parents. She knew her parents would never have been able to keep it from her if they hadn't thought everything was all right.

Steps on the stairs. Not much time had passed. Monte came in with the water jug from the refrigerator and two aspirin tablets. "Take these and drink plenty of liquids."

"Did you call?"

"The Chink doctor? Yes. I told you he wouldn't come out here. He said he would phone a prescription to the pharmacy in that little town—can't pronounce it—up the road. I'll go now and pick it up. You stay in bed."

With difficulty, Sara managed to swallow the aspirin and some of the water. Then she threw herself on the pillow and stared miserably at the ceiling.

She wanted to believe that he hadn't really called. That David really didn't know she was ill. But that was only more wishful thinking of the sort she had indulged in yesterday when her mind furnished her with all those excuses about busy telephone lines, a phone out of order, a medical emergency.

The aspirin made her sweat. Her fresh nightgown became damp quickly and her hair was sticky on her neck. As she gathered it and lifted it out on her pillow she remembered David's fingers lifting her hair that night, and the way they had lingered against her neck.

No doubt by now he was as embarrassed about everything as she was.

She had heard the Saab leave and in half an hour or so it came back. Monte came upstairs pretty soon with a pitcher of lemonade, which he set on the bedside table.

"Here is the penicillin. You're to take one now and then one every six hours."

Sara put out her hand and he shook a white tablet from a small envelope where she could see David Choy, M.D. scrawled with the date and dosage. But maybe David had not . . . Cut it out, let the dream die. She reached for water and swallowed the penicillin.

"Thank you." She tried to put some graciousness into it. There was no use in trying to pretend she liked him, but she didn't have to antagonize him. If Mr. Nielsen thought well enough of him to be associated with him she supposed he must be respectable, at least.

He was pouring lemonade into a glass. "Try to drink as much today as you can."

"You mustn't feel that you have to stay here and take care of me. If Mrs. Nielsen knew I was sick I'm sure she would see to it that—"

"She knows. I told her. Don't expect to see her or anybody else from that part of the house. She is terrified of germs for fear her son might catch something."

"I want to get out of here."

"You will. Just take that penicillin and you'll probably feel pretty good tomorrow. I don't think you've got anything very serious wrong with you." His smooth face was totally devoid of expression as he looked down at her. "What shall I fix you to eat?"

"Nothing. I'm not hungry."

He went downstairs.

Early in the afternoon Sara could tell that her fever was beginning to rise again. She drifted in and out of delirious sleep. Rita was one of the feathered Bird People and she was flying after her calling, Sweetie, sweetie. A voice whispered, *She hasn't a chance.* But that was David's voice and he was laughing. She ran after him, trying to cry out that it was all a mistake. She caught hold of him, but when he turned, his face was that of the tree with its mouth wide open. Gray fingers reached for her throat, strangling.

She woke, wondering if she had cried out when she saw Monte Rivers standing beside her bed.

"Do you want something?"

She mumbled that she always had delirious dreams when her fever was high.

"I think you'd better take some more aspirin."

She took it.

"How does your throat feel?"

"Maybe a little better."

"Do you want something to eat?"

"No, nothing."

"Finish the lemonade and I'll bring you something to eat later. You have to eat if you want to keep your strength up. How about some eggs?"

"All right." She wanted to keep her strength up so she could leave.

When her fever went down she threw off the covers, sweating again and restless. She tried again to read, but it was impossible to keep her mind on the book.

Bird People. Who were the Bird People? Were they some kind of kooky, far-out cult? Could there possibly be a connection with some sort of disease—like parrot fever? She remembered having been tested for something at the hospital that was connected with birds. Pigeons? Yes. Oh, it was all so mixed up and crazy that she wasn't even going to try to figure things out.

She put on her robe and sat on the edge of the bed when she heard Monte coming upstairs. He had a tray with her supper. She saw scrambled eggs.

"How do you feel?"

"A little better."

"You look as if your temperature might be down. Have you been taking your penicillin?"

"Yes, of course." Didn't he know how badly she wanted to get out of here?

Rita had said he was a genius and he really had to be one, she thought, to have turned eggs into honeycombed plastic sponge. There was toast and she made herself eat all of it. There was tea and she drank it, the warmth a little comfort to her throat .With her fork she prodded at the clods of yellow. Oh, boy. And the pin on the map at home still said she was at the Aloha Nui.

Well, she could put this little human-interest episode into the talk to her mother's book club. "There I was," she would say to all the familiar faces, "with this guy who looked like Marlon Brando taking care of me—and taking about as much interest in me as the real Marlon Brando would have done . . ."

How they would clap, beaming. Oh, my, that *sweet* Sara Moore. Her mother would be all flushed with pride when she told her father how good her talk had been. Her father would be glad only that she had been restored to them safely so they could continue their threesome life together. Bless him, he would plan camping trips to keep her happy.

It should be enough.

Still-faced, Sara lay on her bed and watched the sky as it turned to a soft pink like the Seven Sisters rose her mother had over the back door. The pink deepened to coral, which became a flat sea for a purple ship which grew larger, coming closer. Sne didn't want to know how to read the clouds.

When the sun had burned the last of the light from the sky she began to dread the night.

The ancient tree had begun its patient scraping to get her attention. She was afraid of that tree. All night it would whisper, seem to be trying to get into her room. And the gnarled branches would take on the look of that face again.

She knew she was a coward to be afraid of that tree.

Or a fool, to be afraid only of that tree?

There was something else, something she did not understand. Should she lie here and use this wakeful time to put them together, add them up?

Later. She must try to put worries out of her mind so she would be able to sleep tonight and be well tomorrow. When it was time for her penicillin she took a double dose and some aspirin. Her fever receded again and she slept.

CHAPTER TWENTY

The knocking on her door was impatient. "I've got your breakfast."

Sara said drowsily that she wanted to sleep. She heard the tray rattle as it was set down, then steps descending. In a minute the Saab drove away.

She lay on her bed, languid, devoid of all desire to move. She knew she should get up and try to eat something if she intended to get out of this house today. She knew also that it must be about time to take another dose of penicillin.

She dozed for a bit, and when she opened her eyes again and looked at her watch it was almost ten.

Quickly then she sat up and stretched. The aching feeling had gone. She took her pill with a little water and found that her throat was scarcely sore at all. The illness she'd had in the spring had not responded to penicillin, she remembered, so whatever she had had these last couple of days must not be anything to worry about. A little dizzy, she unlocked her door, picked up the tray, and took it to a chair beside the window.

It was her own fault that everything was cold. She drank the orange juice, nibbled at the toast, pushed aside the coffee, and only looked at the egg, which was another masterpiece: the edges were like fried lace and the yolk was still slimy on top. But be fair; she should be grateful that he did things for her at all. Perhaps he felt he had to fill in for Rita in her absence. Or had Mr. Nielsen said . . . ?

Sara was completely unable to imagine anything that the strange Mr. Nielsen might have said. The whole situation with its strange cast of characters was too much for her present state of mind: dear Chris who was reconciled to dying; Mrs. Nielsen who laid offerings on strange altars; Rita, the child beater, who had gone to see the Bird People.

And David Choy. Oh, don't forget David Choy whose children she had imagined having! She had looked into their faces. She had moved her parents to Hawaii. She knew that she might make her father understand about the little fling with Joe Egan, but she knew she could never make him understand that within the first hour of meeting David Choy she had known she would marry him if she could.

A telephone started ringing downstairs. It sounded as if it came from Monte Rivers' room. She had known there must be one there, but this was the first time she had heard it ring. She wasn't going to try to answer it; it wasn't for her.

The ringing went on. She put her tray down on the floor. It could be for her. She stood up, a little light-headed, and put on her robe. Holding onto the banister, she started down the stairs. When she reached the bottom the ringing stopped.

§ *159*

It could hardly have been David calling after all this time. But there was a chance that it was his nurse, making a routine call to inquire about the patient; she could have secured this number from the main part of the house. Sara knew it was unlikely, but it did suggest a logical, face-saving excuse for calling him. She would tell him she wanted to thank him for prescribing the penicillin. She would be very casual: *Just thought I'd say thanks, David.* What a see-through thing that would be. Like something Eloise might dream up.

Her pulse had quickened and she was about to lose her nerve. *Don't think about it twice or your pride will never let you do it. And pride is mighty cold comfort.*

He might say, Oh, Sara, I tried and tried to call you, but . . .

No fantasizing. Just do it, Eloise.

The door of Monte Rivers' room was locked. What treasures were in there, for heaven's sake? Or was it only the phone that for some reason he didn't want her to use? She was already on her way up the stairs to get her own key and try it in the lock. It didn't fit any better in his lock than it had in hers, but after a few tries she had his door open. If he should come back and find her in here she would say calmly that she had heard the phone ringing.

She was much less calm when she sat on the untidy bed and reached for the phone, trying to remember what she had planned to say to David. Her heart was sending dizzying waves of blood into her head as she found the telephone book and looked up his number.

"May I speak to Dr. Choy, please?"

"Oh, I am sorry, but Dr. Choy is just leaving his office for the day."

"Oh. Well, I just wanted to thank him for doing a favor."

"He has to make a speech at a medical meeting in Honolulu."

It didn't sound like the same girl she had talked to on Saturday. "Who is calling, please?"

"This is Sara Moore."

"Oh—oh! Please hold, Miss Moore. Dr. Choy said that if you were to call—let me see if I can catch him."

Sara heard David say he would go into his office to take the call. She heard a door close and then, "Sara, Sara. I've been out of my mind. Where did you go?"

"I didn't go anywhere. I've been right here at the ranch. Waiting for you to call me, hoping—"

"Oh, no." He groaned the words. "I called the ranch Sunday morning earlier than I said I would—around ten. I was told you had left."

"Oh, David, who—?"

"One of the servants—he came back to the phone and said you had gone. I waited and waited, thinking you would get in touch. And then I started calling the hotels. Yesterday afternoon I called Mr. Nielsen and tried to find out something from him, but he had been drinking and I don't think I even made him know who I was. I tried to find Rita and found she had gone to Honolulu. I thought maybe you had gone with her."

"Oh, David, David." Emotions, questions were crowding, but there wasn't time enough to say everything. "You didn't prescribe any penicillin for me?"

"Oh, my God, no. What kind of crazy mix-up is this anyhow? Somebody is going to give me some answers. How did you get . . . why did you need . . . are you sick?"

"No, not now. I mean, it wasn't much of anything. There is a doctor staying here and I guess he . . . anyhow, I'm better now."

"Good. And I'm glad there's a doctor there. Sara, look, I wouldn't be going to Honolulu if I didn't have to make a speech this afternoon. I've got to hang up in a minute or I'll miss my plane, but I will be out there the first possible minute after I get back."

"I was planning to leave this afternoon just as soon as I felt up to it."

"No." His voice was firm. "Absolutely not. You stay right there and take it easy. I want to pick you up there so there won't be any more screwed-up misunderstandings about where you are. My meeting will last all afternoon, but I'll catch the first plane. I still have that patient in Coronary Care so I'll check by there first and get it over. Then I will come to the ranch. Be packed and ready. I'll try for seven. Sara, if I didn't think you were all right out there—"

"Oh, yes. I'll be all right now."

Sara put back the phone and got to her feet with a faintness that was euphoric. She locked the door and floated out into the living room. Oh, thank God, she had called him! Monte Rivers must have told the servant she wasn't here—no doubt Rita's ridiculous high-handed orders: *Don't let her go out with anybody. She could be knocked down, robbed, raped* . . .

She sat down suddenly in a living-room chair, conscious of weakness. It had been two days since she had eaten a real meal. At the moment she wasn't able to think very sensibly, but she did know she ought to go into the kitchen and find something to eat.

She found eggs, milk for a wonder, made an eggnog with plenty of sugar, and drank it. She rinsed out her glass, determinedly ignoring the rest of the dirty dishes.

Back up on her bed again she was aware that she was pretty shaky. It would be good to obey David's orders and take it easy for the rest of the day. By tonight she was sure she would be completely well.

The little car came back. Monte Rivers made noises down in

the kitchen that sounded as if he was unpacking groceries.

He came upstairs. "So you're still in bed. That's good." He glanced toward the tray. "I see you didn't eat very much of your breakfast. I bought some soup for your lunch—maybe that will suit you better. You do have to eat, you know. Are you feeling better today?"

"Much better." Sara met his impassive gaze with one of her own. She disliked him, wouldn't trust him, but to get answers to her questions she would have to admit she had been in his room. Anyone with his obvious hostilities was bound to have hang-ups, and a somewhat abnormal need for privacy might be one of them. It was also possible that he had lied about the prescription because she had wounded his professional pride by asking for another doctor. Since she had to spend several more hours here she wasn't going to fight with him.

He picked up her breakfast tray. Over his shoulder he said, "By the way, Rita will be back this afternoon. I'm picking her up. I've not had time to do anything about picking up your mail, but—"

"Don't bother."

Sara preferred to pick it up herself. There was still a bit of question in her mind about the other letter. David would drive her down there.

David. She broke every vow she had made and dreamed as recklessly as she had in those first hours after being with him. If only he had not been told she had gone. But that wasn't worth bothering about now that everything was turning out so happily. The only thing that bothered her now was that old tree scratching on the screen. From time to time it seemed to give a convulsive shudder. She wished it were not quite so much like a person. She wished she had a radio to drown out that persistent sound.

For lunch, beef-vegetable soup. She was hungry. Monte stood

looking at her as she started to eat. "Well, you must be feeling better if your appetite is back."

"I'm really hungry."

"Good. But don't get any ideas about getting out of bed—you could be right back where you started if you aren't careful. I'll bring up a pitcher of lemonade before I go out so you won't have to go downstairs."

Such solicitude. "What time does Rita's plane get in?"

"Four twenty-nine. But I'm leaving here early because I've got a lot of things to do."

She washed her sticky hair and took a sponge bath. Monte came up while she was in the bathroom and called in to tell her he had brought her lemonade. "You just stay up here and rest. And Rita will do the dishes—don't you try to come down here and do them."

"Don't worry."

It was a relief to hear his car drive out. She had more time to herself now than she had expected to have, and as she dried her hair by the window she made a sudden decision. She was feeling almost completely recovered now, and she was going to end her visit at the Ulewehi Ranch in proper fashion. She would thank Mrs. Nielsen and say goodbye to Chris. Mrs. Nielsen had been kind to her, and poor Chris was a love.

She dressed then in a cool blue knit, and twisted her hair, still a bit damp, up on top of her head. She smiled as she put on glossy pink lipstick. Her delicate features were still a little wan, but her blue eyes were shining. In just a few hours she would be seeing David. *Oh, God, I am so happy!* She hummed as she ran down the stairs. There would be plenty of time to pack her clothes later.

Quickly she walked along the dark hall and then her steps slowed. It hardly seemed right to go, as she had done that first morning, down the long hall that led to the wing containing the servants' rooms—they might be resting at this time of day. It would be stupid to go around the house to the front door and ring the bell as if she were someone making a formal call.

Sara hesitated with her hand on the latch of the garden door. The garden was a private place. She had been made to feel like an intruder both times she had gone in here. And there was something about the place that she disliked very much.

Carefully she pushed open the door and looked down the long lanai that led to the main part of the house. No one was in sight. How still it was. How oppressive and funereal the scent of the flowers. She stepped out from under the monstrous vine, which seemed to have grown noticeably larger in just these few days.

Chris lay, half reclining, on a chaise longue in the only spot of sun. She had a moment of wondering how he could breathe in this closed-in place. He saw her, sat up. She looked away quickly from the sight of quite awful scars on his chest. He fumbled for his shirt and put it on.

"Sara! I thought you had gone."

"I've been sick."

"I know, but they told me you had left yesterday." He finished buttoning his shirt, stood up.

Sara spread her hands in a puzzled gesture. What was the matter with everybody around here? "No, I've been right here, Chris, but I'm leaving around seven. I wanted to tell you goodbye. I thought I would thank your mother too for letting me stay here all this time."

"My mother is lying down right now."

She remembered what Monte Rivers had said about Mrs. Nielsen's fear of germs. "Oh. Well, I won't bother her. And I won't come close to you, Chris. I don't want you to catch whatever I've had."

"Oh. Well, right."

He wasn't acting like himself. Sara thought maybe he had been embarrassed because she had seen the scars on his chest.

"There's a special reason now why I can't take chances."

"A special reason?"

"We're leaving tomorrow."

But that didn't explain anything.

Chris leaned against a tree a little distance from her, tore off a piece of loose bark, and examined it carefully. "We're catching an early plane out of here for Honolulu and then going on to San Francisco."

"You're *catching* a plane? But I thought your father had his own jet."

"Yes. Not using it this time for some reason." He turned suddenly and put his forehead against the tree trunk, his head moving back and forth and his fist pounding. "Oh, God, God. Sara, I might as well tell you. They've found a donor."

She stared. "A—what? A donor?"

"A heart donor."

"Heart? But I didn't know that you . . . Chris, I thought you had asthma, emphysema—some sort of chest thing—"

He laughed tiredly. "Some sort of chest thing—right, oh, right. It's my goddamned heart. Ever since I've been born it's been my goddamned heart."

She said words that she knew were stupid. "But—somebody has to die before—"

"Yes. Of course. Somebody is dying. This person has got something fatal, terminal. Whatever it is, whoever it is. I don't want to know if it's man, woman, or child. There is something so—so ghoulish about waiting for somebody to die and then"—he sucked breath between his clenched teeth—"taking . . ."

Sara tried to get past her shock and think of some good words to say. There weren't any good words.

He gave his attention to the scaling bark of the tree again, stripping it off in pieces and throwing it to the ground. "Just now I was lying over there thinking and—oh, my God, I don't see how I can go through with it!"

"Your parents—do they think that it's—?"

"Yes. Oh, yes. My mother was so excited it was pitiful when she first heard about it on Sunday. But last night she saw a ring around the moon. She believes in all the signs. She's scared now. And she cries. My father just drinks, the way I've never seen him drink before, and I can't get him to talk much about it."

For the second time since she had known him, Sara had the almost uncontrollable urge to go to him and hold him close in her arms. She was on the verge of weeping. "Chris, Chris, I'll say all the prayers I know. And I'll see you sometime again, and you'll be well, and—"

"What is it like, Sara? I have never been well." His tortured breathing was plainly audible from where she stood. "This isn't living."

"So if there's a chance—"

His thin face brightened a little. "There is. I guess the odds are lousy, but there is a chance. My father says the tissue match is as perfect as it ever could be unless I had an identical twin. He has been in touch with the man who knows all about it. And the blood is right—that's always been the big problem every time I've had an operation. I've got B-negative blood."

"You have? Well, so have I!" She said it eagerly, glad to have found some good words to say. "Chris, you tell them that if you need any of my blood just to send for me. I'll come. I mean that."

"Sure. I know you mean it."

A voice called from a distance, "Son, where are you? We have to go."

"Just a minute, Mother." He said to Sara, "We have to go to the hospital every week for some kind of dumb test. I may not see you again, but will you write to me?"

"All right. Oh, sure, I'd love to write to you, Chris. I'll write you lots of letters."

"Aloha, Sara."

"Aloha, Chris. Maybe it won't be as bad as you think."

"I know what it will be like. It will be pure hell. Just ordinary heart surgery is hell. I've had it five times." He held up his hand with all fingers spread.

The garden seemed to close about her. The wide flower faces seemed to lean, laughing, expelling their sick sweet breath in her face. "How many times, Chris?"

"Five."

When she went back down the dark corridor her hands touched the walls cautiously as if she were blind, or very old, or very ill. She went through the kitchen and up the stairs to her room and sat down at her dressing table.

The freckles stood out on her pale face. She saw that a red blossom had fallen on her hair and was caught in it. She pulled it loose and the soft, half-rotten petals bled on her fingers. She tried to throw it into the wastebasket, missed, and got up and dropped it in carefully. It seemed important to get the bleeding thing out of her sight.

She stood then looking at the flower's blood on her fingers.

Five open-heart operations, Chris had said.

Five open-heart operations, Dr. Durham had said. That day in the hospital he had held up his five spread fingers as Chris had done. What else had he said that day? That the desperate father would build a wing on the hospital. That he would pay anything for a heart for his son.

Outside the window the old gray tree was clawing now in agitation at the screen. There was a mouth. It was open in that wide silent scream.

She was very much afraid.

But not of the tree. At last, not of the tree.

CHAPTER TWENTY-ONE

An idea was struggling to be born. It grew second by second, becoming a monster as it shouldered its way, tearing into Sara's world.

She went to the bed, knowing she must lie down or fall down. She was panting as if she had been running. She felt a little sick as her shaking hands wiped sweat from her face.

This is the girl. She hasn't a chance. The whispering voices were harsh in her memory.

Had that illness come back on her now after a remission that those who loved her had cruelly allowed her to enjoy?

She could not believe that. And she was not ill now except for the sudden blow dealt by her fear. She sat up, trying to calm herself, trying to think sensibly while all the little things added up to their stunning total.

She thought of her parents. She would call her father: *About your dream—did you dream that I went to the hospital again?* Stupid, stupid. That wasn't the place to begin. Whatever she did, she must not call her parents.

Call Dr. Durham. Come right out with the question: *Dr. Durham, just tell me one thing—do I have a terminal illness? I am perfectly calm. You can tell me.* She pressed her fists against her forehead, trying to decide what else she would say to him. *Dr. Durham, I didn't win any contest. I was brought here.*

He would ask her how she knew.

Little things, she would say. *Lots of little things have happened since I came here.*

What things?

Well, what? Sara tried to organize the numbing fears that threatened to halt all rational thinking.

She was sure now about the contest. But she could not prove it. She was sure now that there never had been any reservation made for her at the Aloha Nui Hotel. But she could not prove that either.

She couldn't prove that Rita had torn up her postcard to Dr. Durham, nor that a letter from him had been burned. But it was logical enough to assume that they wouldn't have wanted her to have any contact with a doctor at Brill Hospital. A doctor who might know some things, remember them later, putting them together in a way that until now she hadn't had sense enough to do.

It must have been Monte Rivers and Mr. Nielsen who whispered together that day at the hospital. Monte must have been working there then, with access to her records.

All guesses. Not one of them based on anything that she had seen with her own eyes. She couldn't call Dr. Durham with a wild bunch of hysterical conjectures that her mind had built to almost unimaginable horror. Maybe all they wanted was some of her blood. She would give blood so gladly for Chris—she had told him that. She tried to calm herself with that thought. Certainly before she called Dr. Durham she had to find something definite to tell him.

It was not yet three-thirty. She had quite a bit of time before Monte and Rita could possibly get back. She was going to see what she could find in that bedroom.

For the second time, Sara took her key and went downstairs to unlock Monte Rivers' door. She searched his desk. None of the drawers held anything of significance except for a deep file drawer where she found two boxes of stationery. One was full of envelopes, and the other was full of paper, that heavy, crackly letterhead that said that Rita Gomez was Public Relations Director for the Valley Isle Construction and Finance Company.

Even before she picked up the telephone book, Sara was fairly certain that she would not find a listing for any such company There were a dozen or more Valley Isle listings, but none for a company by that name. She compared the number on the stationery with the one on the telephone; they matched.

Was it possible that the Valley Isle Construction and Finance Company existed only in this room? Was this all there was to the "company" she had called that day when she sat at the kitchen table with her parents?

It was possible. Clever Rita Gomez. Clever Monte Rivers. They did things so well. Having all that paper printed for just one letter. Stealing, she didn't doubt, the prestigious name of Dillingham and suggesting that her father check it out.

She had to try to be clever too.

Carefully, Sara went through the drawers of the chest so as not to disturb the piles of clothing—not that they were neat. She didn't know what she was looking for. Some correspondence, perhaps. She had to have something more to tell Dr. Durham.

Her quick fingers went through all the pockets of the clothes that hung in the closet. There was nothing of interest in them: loose change; a cigarette lighter; a couple of travel folders about South America.

A small black bag, apparently a doctor's bag, sat on the closet floor. It had a combination lock and she couldn't open it. Two travel bags sitting beside it were empty.

She looked about the disorderly room, not knowing where else to search. Had Monte locked the door only to keep her from using the telephone? She had a strong hunch that there must be another reason.

With a sudden inspiration, she went to the desk again and lifted up the boxes of stationery. Underneath was a manila file folder. She drew it out.

It was thickly packed with articles from medical journals, most of which had been Xeroxed. There was also the copy of a chart from Brill Hospital.

The words and symbols under any other circumstances would have been meaningless. But the dates were there and they coincided meaningfully with her stay in the hospital last spring.

She was the white female, age twenty-five, with B-negative blood, whose name had been clipped from the top of the chart.

Sinking to her knees, she looked at the articles, pages and pages of them. Most of them were about tissue typing and compatibility. There wasn't time to read them. If she'd had a year she wouldn't have understood them.

One short paragraph was easy to understand even though it was written for doctors. It had to do with getting permission from next-of-kin for organ transplants. Four out of five relatives gave permission.

Sara became aware that she had started making loud breathing noises the way Chris did.

Now wait. Think sanely. This was all circumstantial. Monte Rivers might be unscrupulous, but he was smart, too smart to think he could get away with a thing like this.

The sheets flapped in her hands as she turned the pages, trying to keep everything in order. More articles, some torn from magazines. A brochure from the Bird Company, manufacturers of respirators.

The Bird People. She felt a little hysterical. Laugh about it later. There wasn't time now.

One magazine article at first glance didn't look as if it belonged with the rest. It was in digest form on cheap-looking grayish paper. It was titled "Is Human Heart Piracy Possible?"

She started skimming. Some of the words began to blur and she forced herself to go back and read with care. The gist of the article was that medical skills had developed so fast that moral considerations and legal rights were in danger of being left in the lurch. A sort of medical Mafia was not beyond the realm of possibility. Even though all hospitals had a ruling that before a heart could be removed a qualified team of doctors must declare irretrievable brain death, high stakes and ghoulish human greed might by-pass the regulations with scant risk of detection.

And then she read: "It is conceivable that the ill-fated donor, selected on the basis of blood and tissue compatibility, could be rendered unconscious by drugs or a blow on the head—this later to be passed off as having resulted from a car accident, a diving mishap, or a fall from a horse. No great amount of surgical skill would be needed to puncture the spinal cord and inject air under pressure, thus causing hemorrhage in the brain stem and, within minutes, brain death. But the heart would go on beating during transportation to the hospital where the recipient waited if the patient could be kept breathing by means of the simplest respirator ..."

Sara's own heart was beating with such loud thuds that the Saab could have driven in and she wouldn't have heard it. But her watch told her that she had about an hour before she could expect Monte and Rita to be here. Long enough to call Dr. Durham. Long enough then to get out of this house.

She sat on the floor beside the telephone with some of the pages spread out around her for quick reference. She dialed the operator.

"Aloha!"

Beautiful Maui. All sunshine and flowers and smiling people. In the dark terror of her mind she had forgotten where she was.

"I want to speak to Dr. Gilbert Durham in St. Louis, Missouri. No, I don't have the number or the address." It was eight o'clock there. She prayed he would be home.

She could hear St. Louis information give the number. In less than a minute, she heard the miracle of his voice.

"Sara Moore! You really dropped from sight! I've not even had a postcard."

"I sent one, but—"

"Did you get my letter?"

"Yes—I mean, no. It came, but—"

"You're upset."

"Yes. You've got to tell me something. It's very important. Dr. Durham, my illness—that thing I had in the hospital—is it terminal?"

"Is it—*what?*" He gave a disbelieving laugh. "I don't have the foggiest notion what you're talking about. Of course it's not terminal. You are well. You're my healthiest patient."

She drew a deep breath. "Oh, good. Oh, thank you—"

"Listen, what made you start worrying about that?"

Knowing that she couldn't take much time, she tried to explain too fast about Monte Rivers and not winning any contest and finding the articles about tissue matching and heart transplants.

"Sara, wait. You're throwing too much at me too fast. You aren't making sense. Talk more slowly."

"I don't have much time. I found an article about heart transplants. It's about what a person could do to—well, listen—" She read him the part about injecting air into the spinal cord and causing brain death. "Is that possible?"

There was a pause. "Well—yes, I guess so, theoretically. Only it's pretty far-fetched. I can't imagine any situation where a person would really try to get away with a thing like that. Sara, this doesn't sound like the girl I know—getting so scared just because you have read some wild, crazy article in a magazine—"

"I found my chart. It's here in front of me. My chart from Brill Hospital."

"Your *chart?*" His voice sharpened. "That's impossible. Which chart? How did it get there?"

"It has my bone marrow differential count—hematologic findings—something about histocompatibility. Monte Rivers had it. I think he got it at the hospital. I think he must have been a doctor there."

"Oh, Sara, Sara, I don't like the sound of this at all. But I don't know the name Monte Rivers. What does he look like?"

"Dark hair, dark eyes, medium tall."

"I can think of about fifty doctors who answer that description. You'll have to be more explicit."

"I think he's Portuguese."

Silence for a few seconds. He said slowly, "Sara, that sounds like a doctor we used to have on Clinical Service. He was taken off that and put into Pathology. And then several weeks ago he was fired.

He's brilliant, but we missed some medication, some instruments. Never could prove a thing, but he was suspected of having a little sideline going. But his name wasn't Monte Rivers—it was Manuel Rivas. Same initials—people usually keep the initials when they change their names. Listen, Sara, if you're involved in any way whatsoever with Manny Rivas—"

"I am! I know it's the same one! I'm here with him. And Chris Nielsen is here—we've got the same blood type. Do you remember Chris Nielsen?"

"The name. It was his father who went around telling everybody he would give any amount of money for a heart for his son. Now, listen to me. Don't panic. I don't know what's going on. I can't think you're in any real danger in a big, first-class hotel. But you get away from there. Can you do that?"

"Yes, yes, I can get away from here. Only I'm not—" But that was too complicated to explain and it didn't matter right now. "All right. I'll leave. He's not here right now. Do you think I should call the police?"

"I guess so. I don't know how much luck you'll have convincing them. The important thing is for you to get out, just get away some place where he can't find you. I don't like this at all, but surely there must be some reasonable . . . I want you to call me back as soon as you can."

Sara promised. With nervous haste she tried to get everything back into the file folder more or less the way it had been. She put it under the boxes of stationery.

Dr. Durham was right. First, get away. It was dangerous for her to wait here until David came for her. He had said he would "try" for seven. But the equipment on the plane would be ready now and . . . Don't think about it.

A glance at her watch told her that Rita's plane would be landing in a few minutes. They would probably take the respirator to the plane and that would give her a little more time. She was simply going to run upstairs and get her handbag and leave. No luggage; that was the least of her worries.

She was going to walk out of here by herself since she didn't know whom she dared trust. Not by the driveway; that was too risky. She would slip out the louvered door and climb the slope past the reservoir, past the grove of trees where she had gone on that first carefree morning. She knew there was a road up there. She would walk until she came to a house with a telephone. Or a passing car might pick her up. She would go then to the hospital. That seemed like a safe, sensible plan. She might get there before David did.

Out in the kitchen, the door of the refrigerator closed.

Sara had been about to leave the room. She stepped back, looking wildly about for a place to hide. To be trapped here . . . how could that car have come back without her hearing it?

She braced herself for the sound of voices. There were none. She tiptoed to the door, listened while footsteps moved in the kitchen. Soft, just a light shuffle. She peered out. It was the elderly maid.

"Missy? Me Mei-ling. Lady send um food. Velly nice. Put um 'way in fligelator. You eat um bime by."

"Oh." Sara went to the living-room door. "Thank you, Mei-ling."

"Me wash dishes? So much dishes."

Sara looked at the bright black eyes, wondering if she should ask Mei-ling to help her. She looked like a kindly person. But she didn't know if she could make her understand. Nor if she dared trust her.

"No. Thank you anyhow, Mei-ling. Please thank Mrs. Nielsen."

As Sara locked the door of Monte's room, she heard the maid's sandals slap down over the three steps and along the corridor.

She ran upstairs. She started throwing a few things into her shoulder bag, wondering if she should take time to sweep everything into her suitcase so that later . . . no. If she didn't get out of here now there might not be any later.

She even decided against taking her shoulder bag. Somebody might happen to see her going up that slope and it would hardly look like a casual stroll if she had that big thing.

She crammed her airline ticket into her billfold. She would lock this door up here. That might give her quite a bit more time. They might think she was asleep. It was twenty minutes of five right now.

A car was coming. Sara looked out the window. The Saab drove around the house and stopped on the lava below.

Monte and Rita got out.

CHAPTER TWENTY-TWO

Numb, Sara sat on the edge of her bed. No thoughts would come. Footsteps were entering the house. Rita was running lightly up the stairs.

"Alo-o-o-o-ha!" She stood in the doorway, all teeth. "How is our little patient? My goodness, we've not been a very good patient, have we? All dressed up as if we were getting ready to go some-where."

"I feel all right now. I thought I might as well get some clothes on."

"Well, you shouldn't have. My goodness, child, sick as you were. Oh, I am very cross with Monte! I have really been bawling him out. Leaving you here alone all this time." Her eyes were busy, going around the room.

Thank God, thought Sara, she had not packed her clothes. It was a very little thing to be thankful for. It was the only thing.

"What have you been doing all afternoon?" Rita's wide smile was outlined in the same orange as the flowers in her dress.

"Well—sleeping, reading. I wrote a letter."

"Have you seen that mess in the kitchen down there?" Her big eyes fastened brightly on Sara's face.

"What mess?" Her mind had begun to work a little. Her safety could depend on their thinking she had not prowled about. She had a frantic moment of wondering if she had left any evidence of being downstairs.

The key! She looked at her door. It wasn't in the lock. What if she had left it in Monte's door? But she could remember locking that door and taking out the key. She couldn't remember what she had done with it.

"Every damned dish in the place is dirty. He's not washed a thing since I left. Sweetie, the sight of it would have given you a relapse. I don't mind doing them, but—that Monte! Wouldn't you think that just once in his life he could rinse something out?"

"You're early. He said when he left that you were coming on the four-twenty-nine plane."

"I had planned to. But I was able to catch the two o'clock from Honolulu instead. We'd have been here lots sooner, but Monte insisted on taking time to try out some silly gadget for the plane."

The respirator. For me. On the private plane. After brain death.

It couldn't be true. Not with Rita looking so calm as she strolled around the room glancing at the crumpled sheets in the waste-basket, adjusting the curtains. At the dressing table she picked up Sara's spray perfume and absently gave the sides of her throat a few squirts as she looked at Sara in the mirror.

"Mm-h, nice. I adore good perfume. Sweetie, now I do think we'd better get back into the little old nightie, and—"

"Oh, no. I've been in bed too long. I thought I might go outside and walk around a little, get some air, some exercise." She said it without much hope.

"Oh, no, no, mercy, mercy. Anybody who has been as sick as you have—Monte told me all about it—taking penicillin and all. We just can't take chances."

Sara lay back. Maybe it was sensible to go along with what Rita said, act as if she were still a little sick, still more than a little stupid. And when the moment came, a quick dash. How fast could she run?

Rita sat on the edge of the bed, taking Sara's hand and giving it a little squeeze. "I'm so glad you're better. You've been such a good sport about everything. While I was waiting for Monte, I called those wretched people at the Aloha Nui and they still don't have anything. But you do have some mail. Maybe tomorrow you and I can drive down there and get it—would you like that?"

Sara looked into Rita's lovely face. What if, in spite of everything, all her dark suspicions were not real, and there were some other explanation that her frightened mind could not at the moment grasp? Rita sitting here like this, smelling of that bon voyage perfume from Woodsriver, smiling like this, holding her hand, could not, surely . . .

Why not? She had all but murdered her own child.

Monte's voice came sharply from the bottom of the stairs. "Who was here?"

Rita patted Sara's hand. "Was somebody here, sweetie?"

"Yes. Mei-ling. The maid. She came up here and said she was leaving some food that Mrs. Nielsen had sent."

"Oh, how *dear* of Mrs. Nielsen. Did you happen to get a chance to talk to Mei-ling?"

"No. I just thanked her."

"Did you see what she brought?"

A trap. She met Rita's eyes, narrowed behind the bright aloha of her smile. "No."

"Well, let me go down and see what the queen has sent us. I'll do up the stinkin' dishes and then I'll bring you a tray."

"I'll come down. I'd rather."

Rita paused by the door. "Oh, I don't think—"

"Yes. I want to try to get my strength back. I'll go out of my mind if I have to stay any longer in this room."

"Well, we'll see."

They would go into a huddle.

It surprised her when, some time later, Rita called upstairs to tell her she could come down.

The kitchen was in order. The food was laid out on a small card table in the living room. They sat together. The platter of food that Mei-ling had brought was bountiful: sliced turkey, a whole avocado, thin bread-and-butter sandwiches, fresh spears of pineapple, wedges of papaya.

Sara forced herself to eat. Monte Rivers—Sara would never be able to think of him by any other name—said almost nothing. Rita chattered a little nervously.

That door behind her, thought Sara, the three steps leading down. She was closest to it. If she pushed the table into their laps, made a dash for it and ran shouting for help, would she have a chance to get far enough to make someone hear her before they caught her? Could their lies cover and explain? Who would care anyhow? Chris would care. Maybe his mother.

She tried to relax. It was only a little more than an hour until seven. They surely had no plans for doing anything so quickly. How did they plan—?

Rita asked if anyone wanted more turkey. Wouldn't it be lovely with such a festive meal if they had some wine!

Sara glanced at Monte's hands, so strong, at his face, the eyes so dark and brooding. Now that she had spoken to Dr. Durham she knew of some of the hostilities that must lurk behind those eyes, eating at his brain, perhaps even justifying what he planned to do. She looked into Rita's bright terrible smile.

"Oh, by the way," said Rita, "something so nice, Sara. Monte was telling me that Mr. Nielsen has very kindly said we could use the swimming pool tomorrow morning. You may not even know they have one. It's out there beyond the guest wing. He's having it filled."

"But—I thought they were leaving in the morning—"

Both pairs of dark eyes met and then turned to pin her. She felt like a butterfly on a board.

Monte put down his fork. "Who told you they were leaving?"

Sara looked from one face to the other. "Mei-ling."

Monte started eating again. "As a matter of fact, they are. Mrs. Nielsen and Chris and Kimo. But Mr. Nielsen will stay on here for a while. The pool will be good exercise for him."

Rita said, "I believe you told me once that you liked to swim, didn't you, Sara?"

"Yes."

Thoughts darted sickly behind what felt like a glass smile. So that was the plan. She visualized herself lying by that pool that she had glimpsed, hair streaming, suit wet, eyes closed. Perhaps there would have been just enough of a blow on the head to knock her unconscious, and then later . . .

Sara bit into a spear of pineapple, told herself to chew. No doubt an ambulance would be called and Monte would announce that he was a doctor. He would have contrived some clever scheme to keep them from taking her to the hospital here, a way to make the flight to San Francisco seem an immediate necessity to save her life.

With Mr. Nielsen, the Island Aristocracy standing by, an act of murder could be made to seem like an act of mercy. And then, she hadn't a doubt, Monte and Rita would leave San Francisco for South America. The brilliant Monte Rivers would be sure to have an agreement that would enable him to get away quickly with what Mr. Nielsen would pay him. No guarantees of success for Chris. No consequences to face. Once her body with its still-beating heart was delivered, they would take off and . . .

Her parents' faces flashed before her, looking at her with love that day at the plane. *Talk to strangers . . . Have the time of your life . . .*

The light in the room seemed to dim a little. Sara reached for her water glass. She never had fainted in her life and this was no time for it.

"Sara! What's wrong with you, sweetie? You look so ghastly all of a sudden—"

Monte Rivers growled that she shouldn't have come downstairs. "I tried to tell you that, Rita—"

"I'm all right. I'll just lie down over here for a minute." She tottered across the room and lay on the sofa. Let them think she was weak; it was true right now. She doubted that she could make it up the stairs. She would lie very still and get her strength back.

She heard Rita clear the table. She washed the dishes and she and Monte murmured together back there behind the partition.

How did they ever think they could get away with anything so mad, so evil? When her parents heard the name Nielsen, as they would surely do, a name she had mentioned more than once in her letters . . .

But she knew her letters must have been censored. They would never have let the name Nielsen get through. They would have scratched out, altered, or simply not have mailed incriminating letters at all.

A thought struck. The relief that surged through her made her feel strong. All she had to do was to walk into that kitchen right now and say boldly, "Remember Dr. Durham at Brill Hospital? I put in a call to him this afternoon and we had quite a little talk. He knows all about you and your plan, Manny Rivas. It's all over. You might as well let me go."

She sat up and wiped her sweating hands on her dress. And then she sank back. What a fool. What did she think he would say, Sure, you can go—?

No, never. He would make a lunge for her and catch her easily. With Rita's help, he would knock her out with a swift needle. And that plane up there, ready and waiting with the Bird respirator, would roar out of here tonight instead of waiting for morning.

A desperate chance for them both, but Sara never doubted that they would take it. They could hardly let her live if they found out how much she knew.

Say nothing. David would be coming soon. She pretended to sleep.

Monte went into the bedroom. Pretty soon he came out and from under her lashes Sara saw that he carried a wastebasket. Sticking out of the top was the edge of the manila file folder and the corners of a couple of boxes that looked like the ones that had held the stationery.

Out in the kitchen he said to Rita, "Hand me that lighter fluid. I'm going to burn this stuff outside somewhere. I think there's a trash burner."

"Good. Yes, there's one on the other side of the garage."

"And then I think I'd better go and have a talk with the boss. This afternoon he was beginning to have some very unnecessary qualms."

"You can handle him."

The telephone in the bedroom rang. Monte had left the door

open and Sara was on her feet instantly. He went past her quickly. He closed the door, but she could hear what he said.

"Yes . . . Yes, certainly I'll tell her . . . Oh, yes, I am sure she will understand, but perhaps you will relay a message for me? Miss Moore will be unable to leave then. I am her doctor and I feel that she must get to bed at a reasonable hour. She has been ill. Please tell Dr. Choy that I will bring her to town tomorrow."

He came out, his dark face expressionless. He glanced at Rita, who had been standing there listening.

Through dry lips Sara said, "You had no right."

"I had every right. Mr. Nielsen trusts me to take care of you. So you had a date apparently. What all went on here this afternoon while I was gone?"

"I—had Mei-ling call him."

He turned to Rita. "Do you know a Dr. Choy?"

She gave a shrug and turned away. "Oh, sure, David Choy. Who was on the phone just now?"

"A nurse. Apparently he's tied up with a patient at the hospital."

"How did she get this number?"

"She said somebody gave it to her at the main house."

Sara said, "But I feel perfectly—"

"How ridiculous," said Rita. "You almost passed out at the dinner table and look at you now. You certainly have no business barging around this island tonight."

Sara lay down again. Monte went on out with the wastebasket. Rita asked, "What's with you and David Choy?"

Sara said dully, "It's just a name my doctor gave me. This place was beginning to get to me this afternoon and—"

Rita was saying soothing words. Sara didn't even listen, her mind in a turmoil as she tried to figure things out. David must have said he would be late—how late? No, no, now he had been told not to come. He would come anyhow as soon as he could. If only he knew what her situation really was. If only he knew that what he had thought of as only a "crazy mix-up" this morning was so unbelievably terrible. He would have no idea: she remembered that when she had told him there was a doctor living here he had said he was glad.

Rita had stopped talking. Sara could tell that Rita's eyes were on her appraisingly. She hoped her face hadn't betrayed her. She wished Rita would relax and leave the room for a minute, perhaps to go to the bathroom, perhaps to freshen her make-up before Monte came back. She could slip out then, run through the dark garden and scream the house down.

Rita stayed where she was. She reached for a newspaper and lit a cigarette.

There must be something she could think of to do while Monte was out! Ask Rita to get her some aspirin from the bathroom? That would take only a few seconds and she needed more time than that. Her mind gave her no inspirations. Half an hour went by.

Sara tried to imagine what Monte was talking to Mr. Nielsen about all this time. What if Mr. Nielsen's qualms had not been so easy to handle? What if he had decided not to go through with this?

In the hospital Monte probably had been able to convince him that she really hadn't a chance. But now he had seen her. Now he must be suspicious that she really wasn't dying. Monte would have to be awfully clever to make his lies stick now.

Her muscles tensed. Hope flared. She sat up and stretched.

"You feeling okay now?"

"Yes. I feel fine."

What would the two of them do if Monte came back with the news that the deal was off—would they just leave? If they couldn't get the money there would be no point in doing anything to her. They didn't know that she had found out anything. In the next few minutes they might be walking out of this place. And she would be free.

"I think you had better go up to bed now, sweetie."

"Not yet. I'm not at all sleepy now. I'd like to read the paper before I go up—I haven't seen one for days."

"It's only the *Maui News*. It wouldn't interest you. But you can take it upstairs if you want to."

"I'll look at it here."

Rita handed it to her and Sara looked at the paper, knowing only that she was holding it right side up and remembering to turn the pages from time to time.

It was almost nine o'clock when Monte walked in the door. He came to stand in front of Sara and stood looking down at her, a muscle jumping in his jaw. "What all did you and Chris Nielsen find to talk about this afternoon?"

Sara tried to keep her upturned face from showing fear. She had never been an actress.

Rita had started to light a cigarette and the flame stopped halfway. "You were talking to Chris this afternoon? How come you lied to me about not having left your room, sweetie?"

"Lied to you?" Sara looked from one waiting face to the other, stalling for time. If she didn't know anything, how would she react? "I didn't really lie to you, I just didn't mention it. I couldn't see that it was any of your business whether I had left my room or not. I couldn't see that it made any difference."

Monte said furiously, "I explained—"

"I was careful not to get close enough to Chris to spread any germs. And we didn't talk much. The poor kid—as you told me, Rita—is pretty crazy. A person can't really talk to him."

"What did he say that sounded crazy?" asked Rita.

"Let me think." Sara folded her hands and tried to steady them against her lips. She was much too distraught to make anything up. "Well, he was talking about birds and stars and things I don't know anything about. And then he started talking about his mother—I don't know—something really crazy about his mother having seen a ring around the moon last night."

"A—what?" said Monte.

Rita said, "Oh, the old Hawaiians used to believe it meant a chief would die—or some such thing. Frankly, I believe that her Majesty is a little bit *pupule* too." Her finger circled her head.

"What else did he say?" asked Monte.

"He said . . ." Sara still couldn't make anything up. She tried to think back but it was almost impossible with Monte's eyes watching her so intently. "He said the moon is in Ku."

"*Ku?*" He turned with an exasperated gesture to Rita. "Is she putting me on?"

"No, no, Monte." She stubbed out her cigarette. "It's just another of those silly old Hawaiian things that you take such a dim view of. Ku was the shark god, the god of human sacrifice. They believed that when the moon is on the wane the supernatural forces are in power—or some such stuff."

Monte said with emphasis, his eyes on Rita, "I don't like it."

She jumped up and patted his arm. "You don't have to like it, or worry about it either. It doesn't mean anything." She put her hand on Sara's shoulder. "Now, sweetie, I do think you should run along up to bed. If we're going to get up early in the morning and have that swim, maybe we all should turn in early."

Sara got up and started toward the stairs. An idea was beginning to take shape. It might not work, but it was worth a try.

She stopped suddenly and looked around at them. "Oh. I just this minute remembered something. Being sick—you know—it just slipped my mind. But tomorrow is my father's birthday."

"So?" Rita had started to go toward the bedroom, but now she came back.

"Well, I forgot to send him anything, not even a card. I thought that if I sent a cablegram now—you know, phoned it in—"

Monte Rivers said, "If anybody ever woke me up at—well, whatever time it is there now—to say, Happy Birthday—"

"No, no, they wouldn't deliver a birthday cablegram until morning. At least, in our town they wouldn't. My father—you don't know him—but he's an awful worrier. He'll worry all day tomorrow if he doesn't hear anything from me on his birthday. He will be sure to think that something is very—odd."

"Odd? Will he?" said Rita.

"Oh, yes. He'll think something is wrong."

Rita's eyes went to Monte and then came back to Sara's face. "What would you want to say?"

"Let me think." Her hand on the banister rail was slick with sweat. *Something about his dream*. But how could she word it so that it would sound innocent?

"I could say, 'Happy birthday, Daddy. This trip is a dream come true.' How many words would I have?"

Rita said she didn't know.

Sara held her breath as she looked from one face to the other. In Illinois, morning came four hours earlier. It was not her father's birthday. The minute he read those words he would be alerted to the fact that something was wrong. There might even be time for him to do something.

"Well, I think that's sweet," said Rita. "Don't you think that's sweet, Monte?"

"Very."

"Why don't you get a piece of paper then and write it down before you forget it?"

"I won't forget it."

Sara clung to the banister. His eyes were steady on her. She could feel the hard beat of the pulse in her throat and wondered if he noticed. "I will pay you whatever it costs. How much do you think it will be?"

"I don't know. But it doesn't matter—I can't send it until morning. The Western Union office won't be open now—it's past nine o'clock."

Sara didn't know whether that was a lie or not, but she hadn't really expected that her feeble trick would work. The effort had drained her of strength, and she didn't know anything else to do but go up to bed. Oh, my parents, she thought, happy now, their fears allayed by that Honolulu telephone call that Rita had cleverly suggested she make.

"I'll be up pretty soon, sweetie," Rita caroled. "You just get ready for bed."

Sara climbed the stairs and went into her dark room. They had begun talking in Portuguese before she closed the door. They knew she was afraid.

Oh, God. Oh, God. Oh, God.

She didn't turn on the light. She knelt by the window and looked out at the blurred stars. The moon did have a ring around it and the air was heavy. The old tree dug at the screen, panting on the rise and fall of the night wind.

David, come. Hurry.

CHAPTER TWENTY-THREE

Like a child, obedient and dull-normal, Sara got ready for bed. Perhaps there was no way now of making them think she wasn't suspicious, but protests might be worse.

She still had that one plus: Rita and Monte had no way of realizing how much she knew. They did not know the extent of her conversation with Chris, and of her own stunned totaling of all the bits and pieces of information. They did not know that she had gone into Monte's room and found the file folder.

For a bit she worried about whether he might have looked through those papers and noticed that they were not exactly as he had left them. But, untidy as Monte was, he probably had not. He would just have been in a big hurry to get rid of all the evidence in case a search should be made here later.

He could not know that she had used that phone in his room to call Dr. Durham in St. Louis.

She thought about her key again and looked around on the dressing table for it. Wherever it was now, she had at least taken it out of Monte's door. It was about the only sensible thing that she could think of that she had done.

She took down the hair that she had put up this afternoon, remembering the way she had felt then. In spite of all the things that should have warned her, she had been full only of happy, mindless anticipation at the thought of seeing David again.

She tore at her hair with a brush, glad it hurt. Why hadn't she risked one extra minute in that room this afternoon to call David's office, or the police, or somebody, anybody? Dr. Durham might have been able to have done something for her by now if she had only had brains enough to take time to explain to him that she was not staying at the Aloha Nui.

Close to hysteria, she slammed her brush down. Go ahead, cry. Cry because you're almost as stupid as those two think you are! That ruse about the cablegram had been so transparent. It had been crazy to think for a moment that Monte would send it!

But David would come. David had to come.

Sara got into bed, not knowing what else to do. She picked up her book and when Rita came upstairs she was pretending to be absorbed in it, hoping Rita would think that the idiot girl's fears were now lulled.

"All tucked into bed. Good. Reading, I see." Rita had a glass of water in her hand.

"Yes. I like to read before I go to sleep."

"Is it a pretty good book?"

"Oh, it's terribly exciting. It's one of those books you just hate to put down."

"You've not gotten very far if it's all that good."

"I'm a slow reader." *Dumb. I move my lips when I read. I'm used to comic books.*

Rita was also ready for bed wearing a filmy nightgown and robe. She had beautiful breasts, heavy, as if she could nurse a child. Her voice was soft, as if she could sing lullabyes.

"I am so glad you are better." She gave Sara's forehead a light, soft touch. "Have you been taking your penicillin?"

"Yes."

"Well, now I want you to take this capsule. It will help you sleep." She held it toward Sara.

"Oh, I won't need anything to make me sleep tonight. I'm really exhausted."

"All the more reason why you should take it. Sometimes we get so tired we can't sleep."

"Oh. Well, thank you, Rita. Just put it down there on the bed-side table."

"Take it now, Sara."

Sara looked at her watch. "It's only nine-thirty. I want to read for a while. I've reached a place where I can't put it down. I just have to finish this chapter."

Rita said gently, "Take the capsule. You'll have plenty of time to finish the chapter."

"Sleeping medicine doesn't agree with me."

"This will agree with you. It's very mild. I'll wait while you take it."

Afraid to protest more, Sara put her book aside, took the capsule into her hand. It was pink on one end and white on the other.

"Well, do snap it up, sweetie. Don't just keep me standing here like this."

If I take it, I may not wake up at all. "You didn't happen to see the key to my door, did you?"

"No. Take it!"

Sara put the capsule into her mouth and reached for the glass. She took a sip of water.

"There now, sweetie," Rita crooned, "in about twenty minutes you'll start feeling just a little bit drowsy. By ten o'clock you'll be dead to the world."

Sara smiled up at her.

"You won't forget to turn off your light, will you?"

Sara shook her head and picked up the book again.

"So it's a pretty good book, eh?"

Sara nodded, opened the book, pretending to be trying to find her place.

"Did you really swallow that capsule, sweetie?"

She opened her mouth to prove it.

Rita left the room.

When the door had closed, Sara took the capsule from under her tongue. It had begun to be limp and sticky. If Rita had stood there for just a few more seconds, the contents would have dissolved in her mouth. She pushed the capsule under the mattress as far as she could reach.

So she had scored one small victory, just one. She was almost but not quite as dull-witted as Monte and Rita thought she was. And now the brain cells they didn't suspect were going to have to save her life.

After a few minutes had passed, Sara turned off her light. More minutes went by. There was silence in the living room below, but Sara was sure Rita was still there.

Sara could almost see her sitting there smoking thoughtfully. She might be wondering if she had been tricked about the capsule. In all probability she would come up to make sure Sara was asleep. She might even try to get her to take another capsule. It was vital to put Rita's mind at rest, make her think that for the next hours she would be fast asleep, no bother.

When the door creaked open, Sara was lying on her back. Knowing that quivering lids would betray her, she had placed her arm over her eyes.

"Sara?" It was just a whisper.

Sara forced herself to breathe slowly and evenly. She did not answer.

Footsteps came softly across the rug. She could smell the cigarette smoke, could feel the warmth of Rita's face as she leaned over her. It wasn't easy to keep up her slow regular breathing as Rita listened. What if, right now, Rita were to—? She braced herself for a quick roll off the bed.

But Rita was moving away from the bed now. Apparently she was satisfied.

No, not quite. The door was being closed softly. On the other side, the key scraped in the lock.

Sara stifled a moan against her palm. She wanted to leap from the bed and pound on the door and scream for Rita to let her out, but she made herself lie still, knowing that any outcry would lose her her small victory.

Rita was crossing the living room quickly. Sara heard her go into the bathroom and then into Monte's room. She strained her ears, listening for sounds of conversation, but there were none. Monte might have gone to sleep. Rita would go to sleep.

But how could they? *How could they?*

Sara waited. Except for the sounds made by the old tree, the night was quiet.

After a while she got up and tried the door softly. It was locked, as she had known it would be. It had occurred to her as she lay waiting that there was a chance Rita had used Monte's key. Her own might still be on the dressing table, overlooked somehow in her earlier search. Surely she must have put it there when she had rushed upstairs after locking Monte's door.

She felt around carefully in the dark. She knelt, moving her hand around the floor. It wasn't there.

Rita must have picked it up when she tried out the perfume. Sara could remember the way the dark eyes had been on hers in the mirror as she stood there spraying the perfume on her throat. At that moment she must have had the key in her hand, planning even then to lock the door tonight.

How could she hope to outwit those two when they were so many carefully thought-out jumps ahead of her?

She had a small inspiration and felt around on the dressing table for a hairpin. Straightening it, she hurried to kneel before the door and started poking through the keyhole. She could tell the key was there; she knew it fit loosely and she believed it might be possible to poke it out. There was a wide crack under the door. Perhaps she could make a loop out of something, maybe the strings from her sneakers, and if the key should fall close enough she might be able to pull it under the door.

The key fell out of the lock. She heard it bounce down a couple of steps.

Fighting despair, Sara went to lean her forehead against the screen of the window overlooking the mountain. A faint light glimmered from the observatory shack. Chris must be out there. Could she wait here by this window, watching for him to come back to the house, and then scream to him?

The thought of her screams awakening Rita and Monte frightened her too much. Before Chris could do anything, they would be upon her.

David might come. David might not come. Somehow she was going to get out of this room.

The old tree was scratching insistently. She went over to that window which she had scarcely looked out of because of the obstructing tree. Her fingers slid along the bottom of the screen feeling for the hook that would let her open it. She found the hook, but the screen had been painted in, or nailed. She couldn't budge it, and she was afraid to make any noise pounding.

A bony knuckle of the tree had worn a small hole in the screen, as if to show her that the screen was rotten. The tree leaned, swaying in the breeze, sinister no longer, as if to show her that the old limbs, silver in the faint moonlight, were strong enough to hold her.

She wished she could turn on a light, but she dared not risk it even for a few seconds. One of them might be lying awake down there. Even though their room was on the other side, their door might be open and the briefest reflection of light could be disastrous.

She felt through her suitcase and found the only dark clothes she had brought with her, jeans and a navy pullover and sweater. She put on her sneakers, her mind seizing upon and discarding ways of getting through that screen. She knew she could not tear it apart with her hands.

Once she had seen her father cut screen wire with a big pair of shears. She had no shears. She had razor blades. Too dangerous. She could break a glass in the bathroom. No, no. But she had those cheap little jeweled manicure scissors Brenda Jean had given her. She found them.

Someone was walking across the living room. Monte. He might have heard her moving around up here although she had tried not to make a sound. He could have changed his mind, deciding not to wait until morning to do what he had to do.

She wondered if she could wait by the door and bring a chair crashing down on his head. Run then . . .

But the steps continued across the kitchen. He opened the door and went out. Standing back from the window, Sara saw him get into the Saab and drive away. He must have been lying down there awake and suddenly remembered something that had to be connected, checked, tested.

She should have an hour, maybe more, before he came back.

Sara started cutting the screen, the tiny scissors twisting and slipping in her hand. It was maddeningly slow, but the cutting made less noise than her dry-mouthed breathing.

When the dulling, curved blades had scalloped through a few inches of the screen she discovered that in places it crumbled to rust. She dropped the scissors and started tearing and twisting with her hands.

Putting one knee on the sill, she thrust her head and shoulders through the torn screen and reached with both hands for a firm grip on the old tree.

Like a grandfather, it held her as long as it could in its trembling limbs while she climbed down. A branch broke with a soft, splintering crack as she was about to swing the last few feet to the ground. She fell.

For a little while she lay there, waiting for the light that would surely flash inside. No light came on. She could hear nothing except the gasps of the old tree and her own harsh breath. A cut on her right hand bled warmly. But she was out of that house.

She ran then along the side of the house. There were no lights in the servants' rooms, but the service area between the house and the garage was floodlighted brilliantly. She streaked across it, knowing that her hair must stream like a torch on fire.

When she reached the darkness of the other side of the garage she crouched for a moment, listening. From here she saw a few lights in the main part of the house. It looked as if someone was sitting on the broad lanai in front, but with all the vines and shrubbery she could not be sure.

It didn't matter. Ahead of her was the little path she remembered leading through the tangled bushes. She ran, holding her bleeding hand against her.

The dome of the observatory shack was just ahead of her, and the lighted window showed Chris inside, his thin face rapt as he peered through the telescope at the heavens.

CHAPTER TWENTY-FOUR

Sara flung the door open. Chris stood up, his eyes widening as they went down over her. "Sara! You're hurt! What happened to you?"

She sagged back against the door, hardly able to stand as she tried to get out the necessary words.

"I—found my hospital chart. We—we match, Chris. Monte Rivers is—he's somebody else. He was a doctor at Brill Hospital when we were both there. And he found out—he found out that your father was willing to pay. And he told your father I hadn't a chance. And so—"

He didn't ask a single question. He came toward her with a look that was stricken, knowing. He put his arms around her and held her close. Sara could feel his poor heart beating.

She clung, almost incoherent. "And tomorrow—tomorrow when

you have left, Monte Rivers and Rita are going to . . . there's going to be an accident. There's a respirator on the plane. It's for me. Chris, Chris, I am the donor."

He was trembling with violent shudders. Sara looked up at his tortured face, suddenly afraid that his heart wouldn't be able to withstand the shock of her words. "Chris, I'm sorry, but I have only you—"

"Oh, God!" He shouted the words and gave a terrible laugh that was worse than crying. "Oh, my God, my father!" Her blood on his white shirt, he reached behind her, trying to open the door.

Sara held him. "Wait. Listen, everything is going to be all right now. But don't go to your father—"

"No. I have to get to him—"

She clutched his thin arms. "No, no! Listen to me. What you must do first is call the police. I wasn't sure they'd believe me. But you can make them believe you."

He hesitated, his tarnished-silver eyes dazed, full of anguish.

"That's the only safe way—Chris, believe me! Get to a phone —whichever one is closest—"

He looked down at her, breathing raggedly. "There's one in the garage. Yes, I'll do that. I'll call the police—they know who I am. You wait here. Don't be scared. I'll come back when it's safe. Everything is going to be all right."

He plunged out of the shack.

"Be careful! Don't run!"

Maybe he heard her.

Sara wrapped her sweater around her bleeding hand, turned off the light and went to stand outside.

And she waited.

The slow minutes added up. The haloed moon moved in its own dark sea. All the blurred stars seemed to be trembling, but she knew it was she who trembled with nerves and cold. Her hand still throbbed though it seemed to have stopped bleeding.

Why didn't Chris come back?

She moved a few feet up the slope and sat with her arms hugged close. From here she would be sure to see the lights of the police car when it came up the driveway. They were blue in Hawaii On the road far above she heard the sounds of occasional cars. A plane went over, flashing red and green lights for landing. Far below they were still burning the cane.

The trees and bushes kept her from seeing much of the big house, but the floodlighted area between the house and the garage shone brightly. It was hard to believe that Chris was still on the phone trying to explain to the police. There was a chance that the garage phone wasn't connected. He might have been forced to go into the house to make his call.

She remembered the figure she had thought she saw on the lanai. Suppose that had been his father. Suppose he was arguing with Chris now, telling him she had lied, telling him she was crazy.

Something, *something* must have happened!

Car lights were intermittently visible coming up the lane. David! She had a moment of wild joy as she jumped to her feet. But it wasn't the Jeep. It was the Saab. Time hadn't had much meaning, but it didn't seem possible that Monte Rivers had had time to go to the plane and come back so quickly.

If he saw the broken limb of the old tree . . . if he looked up and saw the torn screen . . .

She couldn't see the car now, but she heard it stop, heard the brake as it was pulled on. Seconds later she saw the lights go on in her room. Fear thickened her blood. Unable to move, she just stood there, not knowing what to do. Should she try to make it to the garage where Chris might still be on the phone? Or run toward the house, screaming for Chris, screaming for all who would hear? No, no! Monte would get to her first.

"Sara—oh, Sara, where are you?" Rita's voice came sweetly, like the voice of a loving mother calling to a child who has played too long in the dark.

The bright beam of a flashlight swung beyond the trees. She ran away from the beam, trying to cover her hair with her sweater. A vine tripped her, threw her flat.

"Sara, sweetie, where are you?" Rita's voice was no closer, but someone was crashing through the bushes back there and the beam of the flashlight swept like a searchlight.

Sara got to her feet and stumbled on to the only hiding place she knew. She felt the thorns of the wild lantana catch on her clothes. She looked for the tree, the fallen tree with the lid of earth like a great door that had opened a few reluctant inches.

She saw it ahead. She squeezed past the roots, dirt falling on her hair, her face. Panting, tasting dirt, she squeezed sideways through the narrow fissure in the rocks.

Inside, it was black with midnight. Her hand groped for the niche where Chris had said he always left a flashlight. Her fingers touched it, closed around it. She knew she dared not turn it on yet. She plunged ahead, forgetting about the low place where they'd had to stoop. She cracked her head, fell with a starburst of pain.

When she opened her blurred eyes she saw that the flashlight had snapped on when she dropped it and lay a few feet away. Dull though her mind was, she knew it was dangerous to show light so close to the entrance. Someone outside could see it. She turned it off, felt around for her sweater, couldn't find it. On her hands and knees she crawled under the low bridge of rock.

When she could stand upright she groped her way several feet back into the cave before she thought it would be safe to risk the light again. She kept her fingers over the beam so that an eerie red glow illuminated the bundles of tapa on the ledge.

But she was not afraid now of the bones of Chris Nielsen's ancestors. The curse was not for her. The thought moved into her mind that they would loan her their rotting tapa to cover herself. She could wrap it around herself and lie on the shelf with the dead.

She remembered that Chris had said there was a hole further along the tunnel which probably led to another cave above. Wouldn't that be safer? It was hard to think clearly. Weak from the blow on her head, she didn't know if she would have the strength to climb up, but she moved forward, trying to see ahead in the red gloom.

Outside, a noise. Sara turned off the light and stood in total darkness.

More noises. The rattle of falling clods of dirt. Someone was coming into the cave. Someone must have been attracted by the glow of the flashlight when she dropped it back there near the opening.

She pressed back against the wall. Water trickled coldly down her back. She could see a flicker of light. There was no time. She gripped her flashlight tight, a puny weapon.

The light wavered on the walls of the burial cave, closer now, full on her as Monte Rivers straightened and came toward her. His lips thinned just a little with satisfaction at having found her.

She clutched the flashlight to her breast. "I found my chart in your room, Manny Rivas."

He scarcely seemed to have heard her. His eyes darted around. He played the light on the ledge.

"I called Dr. Durham at Brill Hospital. He knows."

His eyes resting on her a moment said he did not care. They said Mr. Nielsen would not know until it was too late.

"Chris knows."

His eyes then said he had to kill her. With the beam still on her, one hand reached out for a bundle of tapa on the ledge. He jerked it, and the bones went rattling.

"There is a curse."

For the first time, she saw him smile. He came toward her with the length of tapa spread between his hands.

Sara saw the whiteness, the old geometry of designs that would smother her. When he was almost upon her she whirled, knocking the flashlight from his hands. She ran toward the mouth of the cave.

He came after her. She heard him knock his head upon the narrowed tube as she was crawling through. She struggled to her feet, but he grabbed her hair and dragged her down. She fought off the burial cloth as he tried to cover her.

Outside, a scream. Piercingly, it split the night.

"Auwe! Au-we-e-e!"

Hands still clutching her, Monte Rivers stood up. The terrible shriek, a woman's voice, shuddered through the darkness again. "Au-we-e-e!"

He muttered something and moved past her to stand at the mouth of the crevice. There was more screaming, and now a man's voice in a shout: "Dr. Rivas! Dr. Rivas! Come quickly!"

He did not move.

Sara got to her knees.

And now there came the sound of a car horn and Rita's voice. She called Monte's name and then some hoarse words in Portuguese: "Chris *é morto!*"

He threw down the tapa. He swore. And he was gone.

Dazed, Sara lay at the mouth of the cave for a few minutes. Then, stumbling and ill, she forced her slow feet in the direction of the screaming.

A car started up. The Saab. She caught just a glimpse of it, Rita and Monte inside, as it roared past the floodlights down the driveway.

Was it over? That part of the nightmare?

She took wavering steps, steadying herself on trees, clutching at bushes to help her stay on her feet.

Just this side of the garage she saw Chris Nielsen lying. His mother was on her knees, rocking back and forth and still making that terrible sound of grief for the dead. Mr. Nielsen was there, and Mei-ling and Kimo.

A weeping mist had started to fall, blotting out all those stars that Chris had known the names of.

Like a sleepwalker, Sara moved past them. No one seemed to see her. She found the louvered door, leaned against it for a moment, fumbled for the knob.

Groping along the dark corridor with creeping steps, she came to the end of it, stumbled up into the kitchen and through the living room. All the lights were on. On legs that would scarcely support her, she went upstairs.

The door up there was open and the light still blazed in the room that so strangely had been hers for a while. She saw the old tree beyond the jagged screen.

Each separate thing identified itself, told her that she could remember what it was. Tree. Screen. Billfold, yes, on the dressing table. Clothes, yes, in the wardrobe. Suitcase. Just drop the clothes in the suitcase. The cosmetic case too. A few things in the bathroom.

The bright light showed red on her hand. Blood. That was dirt on her face. Her torn hair was dark with something, maybe blood. She turned from the mirror. Thinking was not for now. Feeling was not for now. She had to leave this place.

It was hard to lift the suitcase. She staggered a little as she half carried, half dropped it down the stairs. She dragged it along the corridor.

An ambulance was out there now. They were taking out a stretcher, running with it.

She heard a car coming with a roar up the driveway. She shrank back into the doorway. Had they come back?

No, a Jeep. David. She remembered him.

She saw him get out, run and kneel.

He stood up, stepped back. He said something to Mrs. Nielsen. Mr. Nielsen was talking to him. The men were lifting the stretcher, carrying it quietly with that long body and the covered face. Nobody spoke.

And then from the great mountain above them came a sound like the marching of many feet. It surged through the trees, closer, louder. Drums rolled. A chanting of voices filled the air. The sound was upon them with a sudden rush.

The Night Marchers had come for the young chief. He was theirs.

It was only the thunder that rolled. It was only the rain that chanted. Sara lifted her face to the beat of it and let it clear her head a little, let herself cry, hurt and full of dull sorrow for the strange dead boy.

Someone was coming toward her through the rain. Someone put his strong arms around her and lifted her into his car. He wiped the rain and the tears from her cheeks.

She touched his face. "David." She could not see him clearly.

He was saying words to her and they drifted, not all of them finding a place in her mind: Sorry to be so late . . . patient in Coronary Care . . . Sara, tell me . . .

She said, "David, David—"

He held a flashlight to her eyes. "I'm going to take you to the hospital."

She said she was all right. All the way to the hospital she kept saying in a thin voice that sounded far away that she was all right.

But it was good to be in the bright safety of the hospital, to have a hand to hold while the authoritative voice speeded procedures in X-ray and lab.

Shock, slight concussion, exhaustion.

It was good to sleep.

Sara awoke early, her vision no longer blurred, her mind clear. Hang onto this clarity, she told herself. Don't let yourself sink back into that other. This is a sheet covering you, not tapa. This sound is today's sound, a radio playing softly beyond the screen that separates you from the patient in the next bed.

This face that was leaning over her now, though scarred and homely under the nurse's cap, held no evil intent. The soft words meant only what they said. "Good morning, Miss Moore. I am Miss Tanaka. Did you sleep well?"

"Yes, thank you." Sara smiled at Miss Tanaka.

"What a pity that you had to have a nasty fall and spoil your nice vacation. I see by your chart that you are from Illinois. Where are you staying?"

"At . . . I'm staying at the Aloha Nui." She was up to no explanations. She opened her mouth for the thermometer and closed her eyes. Miss Tanaka's fingers were light on her wrist. The music had stopped now and the news was coming on. The sound of the radio had been turned up a little.

"Does the radio bother you? I can ask to have it turned down."

"No, no."

"From Washington, the President said . . ."

Good, thought Sara, whatever he said. Hawaii's President, Illinois' President. Civilization and reality were safe about her now. The warm, wet comfort of a washcloth moved over her face, tenderly at the edge of the bruise on her forehead.

"Fourth of July festivities are being planned for . . ." They always had a parade on Fourth of July in Woodsriver. Last year her father had made a speech from the bandstand.

Miss Tanaka said, "I'll brush your hair if you like. Your doctor will be coming in pretty soon. Everybody always likes to fix up a little bit for the doctor."

"Please, yes. I'd like to fix up a bit for the doctor."

The brush made a soothing, scratching sound against the pillow as it reached to draw Sara's hair from under her neck. Her mother had brushed her hair with just such a gentle touch when she was sick.

"Search was begun at dawn today for a private plane reported to have been stolen from the Kahului Airport last night." The brush moved more slowly in Miss Tanaka's hand, and Sara caught hold of it, her eyes wide as they held Miss Tanaka's. "The plane, belonging to Mr. Christian Nielsen of Maui, is believed to have gone down five hundred miles southeast of Hawaii. A freighter reports sighting wreckage which corresponds with the description of the missing plane. Little hope is held for the two occupants whose names are being withheld pending further investigation. And now for a look at . . ."

Miss Tanaka put the brush aside. She reached for a tissue and held it to her eyes. "Please excuse me, but I knew that girl, the one whose name is being withheld."

"You knew her?"

Miss Tanaka blotted tears from the scarred cheeks. "When I came on duty this morning everybody was talking about what happened. You know how fast news travels—"

Sara said, "She was—your friend?"

"Yes. She used to help me with my algebra—I never would have graduated from high school, never would have been able to be a nurse if she hadn't helped me. She was so bright, so beautiful— you wouldn't believe. I never knew why she would bother with me. She didn't have a very good reputation on the island—you know how it is with beautiful girls. But when someone is gone— well, it's nice, isn't it, to have one good thing to remember?"

David came in and Miss Tanaka left. He had spent the night in the hospital. The patient in the Coronary Care Unit had given them a hard time, but they thought now he might make it.

He gave her a tired smile and leaned to kiss her. "Two or three times during the night I came up to see you, wanting to make sure you were all right."

"I'm all right." He had not shaved. He was beautiful. But she couldn't seem to smile. She gestured toward the radio playing soft music now behind the screen. "I heard about Monte and Rita on the news. They might have landed, don't you think, some other place?"

"No, I don't think so. On the way up here I heard somebody talking about what they had heard on short wave—a pretty good description of the Nielsen plane. We'll know more later. Let's wait, and—"

"I want to talk about it now. I need to, David. Miss Tanaka was in here when the news came on. She cried. She said that Rita used to help her with her algebra. I have been trying to think of Rita as somebody who could have helped a poor, scarred girl—"

"Suki Tanaka was in Hiroshima, just a baby when the Bomb was dropped. Yes, I think Rita might very well have wanted to help her."

Sara's head moved back and forth on the pillow. "I can't come to terms with it yet."

"So you're not made of stone—that's all that proves. Neither am I. I called your friend in St. Louis, Dr. Durham—remember, you told me his name. He had been trying to call me. It seems a lot of people are not made of stone where you're concerned."

"You called?"

"Yes. What Mr. Nielsen said to me last night made no sense, but it scared me enough to want to get it cleared up."

"What did Mr. Nielsen say to you?"

"He said everything possible was to be done for you. You'd have had a private room if one had been available. He seemed to think you had a terminal illness. Until I was able to talk to Dr. Durham I thought it might be true."

Sara's blue eyes looked deep into the black-brown ones. "Do you think that Mr. Nielsen ever really believed that?"

"Who knows what we can make ourselves believe when we want to?"

She sighed. She had loved Chris Nielsen. He died for her. Now no comet would ever be named for him.

"I know those parents, Sara, know what that boy meant to them. More, it almost seemed, than if he'd been normal. They have spent these last twenty-one years in a desperate attempt to save him."

"I can understand that, David. I'm an only child."

"Even so, you may want to bring some sort of charges. I don't understand it all very well yet, but you have every right. And when your parents hear—"